The Magic of Cape Disappointment

A NOVEL

Julie Manthey

Copyright © 2015 Julie Manthey
All rights reserved.
ISBN-13: 9781515097884
ISBN-10: 1515097889
Library of Congress Control Number: 2015912466
CreateSpace Independent Publishing Platform
North Charleston, South Carolina

To my family, friends, and fellow coyote spirits everywhere.

The universe is full of magical things patiently waiting for our wits to grow sharper.
—Eden Philpotts, 1918

The Discovery

ccording to all the history books, Meriwether Lewis, of the Lewis and Clark expedition, died childless in 1809. However, the truth is that his daughter, my great-great-great-grandmother Kehlok, turned three years old that year.

My name is Kay Baker, and my brother Louis discovered recently that DNA tests confirmed this family legend. Let me tell you, the extended Meriwether Lewis family is not quite sure what to do with us. Neither is anyone else, because the murder of my great-great-great-great-grandfather, Meriwether Lewis, is one of the biggest cover-ups in history. My family was erased from the history books, disappearing along with Lewis's lost four hundred pages of journal entries. But that is only part of the story—the rest is, well, magic.

❈

Lewis and Clark reached the mouth of the Columbia River where it meets the Pacific Ocean in November of 1805, after eighteen months of grueling travel from their starting point in Saint Louis, Missouri. They traveled with approximately thirty other men through uncharted territory in handmade canoes, on horseback, and on foot until they finally reached Cape Disappointment on the Pacific Ocean. Cape Disappointment itself was named in 1788 by an English sea captain after he missed the Columbia River due to a navigational error and ended up on the cape instead. For generations *before* Lewis and Clark arrived at Cape Disappointment and for centuries *after*, my family has lived in a nearby area that eventually became, in 1852, the city of Ilwaco, Washington.

Meriwether was only thirty-one years old when he arrived at Cape Disappointment. Before leading the Corps of Discovery, Lewis had served as President Jefferson's most trusted assistant and had lived in the president's house at Monticello for nearly four years, since 1801. That Lewis was selected to lead the most secretive, most challenging mission America had ever known at the time was no accident; magic and fate brought him to my ancestor Tamahna on the other side of the known world. Their story is the greatest love story *never* told.

But I'm getting ahead of myself.

New York ❀ November

When my mother called about the news of the DNA results, I was having coffee with my friends Emma and Martina at a little café in Brooklyn near the hospital where Emma worked.

"Hey, Mom, can I call you back later? I'm catching up with Martina and Emma," I explained hastily.

"Kay, the DNA matched! Of course, I knew it would."

"The DNA matched?"

"Oh Kay, you heard me. It's all true—*everything*. And now you have scientific proof. We are direct descendants of Meriwether Lewis."

"Lou will be pleased after battling with that name for years…Mom, can we talk about this later? I'll call you when I get home," I said.

"Of course. Don't forget, Kay, I need to talk to you."

"I won't forget. Bye, Mom." I rolled my eyes as I hung up the phone. "Sorry, guys. My mom," I said as an explanation.

"The DNA?" Emma asked, arching an eyebrow.

"It's a family thing. My mom's researching…something." I wasn't ready to get into this with anybody yet, not even Emma and Martina.

"You never talk about your family," Martina said. "I've known you for four years now, and still only know the basics. You've met my parents twelve times. It's just weird, Kay."

"Whatever. There's not much to say; my family is beyond ordinary," I said casually, knowing that was a bald-faced lie.

"What do they think about you not taking the boards? I can't believe you left medicine for art. You know there will always be a place for you in any practice I'm at if you decide to return," Emma said.

"Thanks, but medicine was my mom's dream, not mine," I said. "Besides, I like being in the city, and I can't believe you're leaving all this for a practice in…Vermont."

"You have a gift for medicine," Emma said. "I know for a fact that you spent more time tutoring others or painting than sitting in class, and somehow you still aced everything. We'd all have hated you for that full scholarship if you hadn't helped all of us pass. You should be a doctor. Vermont is optional."

"I grew up with people telling me that I had to be a doctor because…" I stopped short, avoiding the real reason.

Emma finished my sentence, "Because you're a freak of nature, Kay. Who else in the world thinks that medical school is *easy*?"

"Well it *was* easy. At least five percent of people who complete med school don't become doctors, and you know that. It's not that uncommon. Remember Castellano from second year? He's going to be a reporter on some TV station in Chicago," I said, reminding her of my debate points that we've hashed over several times. Science and math had always come easy to me, so easy that, frankly, I was often bored to tears. I couldn't comprehend why the other students needed a calculator to determine a patient's drug dosage or how anyone could struggle in anatomy. The system of the human body was predictable and systematic, in stark contrast to the subjectivity of art.

"Yes, of course I remember Castellano, and he *barely* passed the program, so he doesn't count," Emma said. "You, on the other hand, graduated first in our class and could take your pick of any residency program in the country. It just doesn't make any sense."

"Look, let's not argue about this *again*. My studio opens tomorrow, and I've already sold a few paintings to some restaurant owner in Baltimore, thanks to Martina. I'm exactly where I'm supposed to be. Can't you just be happy for me?" I asked. Creating a painting that spoke to someone I've never met was far more interesting and challenging than figuring out a patient's diagnosis—something Emma would never understand.

"That reminds me, Kay, I met the best guy to set you up with," Martina said excitedly. "He looks *exactly* like that painting of yours and evidently rides a motorcycle too. And he's a great chef, which—let's face it—you definitely need because you can't cook. Actually, you *shouldn't* cook."

Emma laughed at that comment, having been exposed to my self-proclaimed "gourmet" ramen recipes in med school. "Oh, that sounds promising, Kay," she said encouragingly.

"Oh, please, I'm with Adam. And what do I need a chef for? I have *you* for that," I said, pointing to Martina, whose restaurant I went to nearly daily.

"Yes, of course. My restaurant will never go out of business with you living around the corner. Too bad Tito's married. He's a great chef, and he thinks you're cute," she said.

I laughed. "Ah, but, Tito is no Adam."

Emma chimed in. "So, you and Adam are definitely *on* again then? I can't keep track of you guys these days."

"Yes, didn't you break up with him ten times this month already?" Martina chided.

I sighed. "Only *three* times, and you know that."

"Yes, I remember the phone call at two in the morning. Thanks for that, by the way," Martina complained. I rolled my eyes.

"Adam and I are…on *again*, I guess. I don't know how long it will last, and I definitely won't discuss it with my mom. She was so pleased when we broke up last month. She said it was a sign that I was meant to move home again. Like *that's* ever going to happen."

"Maybe it was a sign…to find someone else, like that motorcycle guy," Emma said.

"You know that I don't believe in signs, superstitions, or magical predictions! Besides, we're not here to talk about *me*. This is Emma's last coffee out before she recklessly deserts us for Vermont," I said, changing the subject.

"I'm going to miss you guys," Emma said. "Kay, I really do wish you'd return to medicine. It seems like you're wasting your talents."

"Or maybe medicine was a waste of my *artistic* abilities," I countered.

"Touché," Martina said. "Not everyone wants to be a doctor, Emma. Give the girl a break. Some of us are happy managing our own businesses." Martina was, of course, referring to owning her own restaurant, after several years working as a food critic. Eventually she decided that with her impeccable taste and a network of the best chefs in the city, she could start her own place and work for herself. We became friends quickly as I basically lived at her restaurant, and she helped sell my paintings by displaying them there. We shared an ambition of working for ourselves and making our own way.

"Yeah, yeah, yeah," Emma said. "You know, not everyone wants to be an entrepreneur either. I much prefer to simply work my hours and then go home, letting someone else worry about the details. The practice I'm joining in Vermont sounds perfect for me, and I'll be their first osteopath, so there's a lot of space for me to carve out my own niche."

"How's the move going? When do you drive out?" Martina asked.

"Everything was in the truck as of late last night, so I have some more paperwork to close out on patients today, and then Ryan and I are off tomorrow. Thank goodness he's an accountant and can live anywhere, because otherwise it would be tough for him to find a job in rural Vermont. We'll be at the studio opening, though. I might hate that Kay's not going to be a doctor, but she's still my friend."

"Gee, thanks. Maybe buy a painting or *ten* for your office to make up for it." I laughed lightly.

Emma shook her head. "Nice try. As long as I still qualify for the roommate discount, then maybe I'll be charitable to help my starving-artist friend whose paintings will soon cost more than a car, especially after that rave review in the *Times*. Uh-oh, that's my pager. I must dash. Thanks for coming all the way over to Brooklyn to meet me. I've been working double shifts for the last few days trying to close out everything and train the interns. At least the new practice will give me a little more time to myself. Vermont has a slower pace. I can't wait to escape the noise of the city."

"I happen to like the noise," I said with a smile, along with a quick hug good-bye.

"Go and save some lives," Martina said dramatically. She had often complained that Emma didn't know how good she had it, even with her double shifts. Martina practically lived at the restaurant to make it a success.

"Think about Vermont, Kay," Emma said. "I'm *serious*."

"I know. You're *always* serious. See you at the studio later," I said.

"Wouldn't miss it," Emma replied.

Martina and I took the subway back toward Harlem. Emma was the last of my med-school friends to leave the city for a practice somewhere else. When I wasn't carving out a few moments for my friends, my world rotated around art openings and the construction crew involved in updating the studio. The constant hum of the city helped me forget the "great prophecy" that my family had as my destiny. I could, and had, chosen my own life here. Finally, I felt free from all the legends and the expectations of my family. Martina and I parted at the subway station; she continued on to meet a potential new organic-fruit supplier. Once home, I opened the window to let in some air and the soundtrack of the city. Collapsing on the sofa, I picked up the phone to call Mom back. I took a deep breath before actually dialing the number.

"Did Emma convince you to move to Vermont?" Mom always started in mid-conversation, and she never said hello. It's as if she just knew when I would call and happened to pick up the phone. She did that with everyone, even before caller ID. Weird.

"No, I'm happy in New York, Mom. So, the DNA thing— what next?" I asked because we had discussed it before and she wouldn't tell me anything, which wasn't unusual. She liked us to find our own path with things—unless that path didn't include medical school in my case. It was the only time she'd insisted, but once I'd finished school, she never asked about it again. My mom was great like that.

"That's for you and Lou to decide. That's not what I wanted to talk to you about," said Mom.

"But that's what you called me about."

"Kay, that's not it at all, honestly!" Mom said, ending with a loud sigh.

"How can you be frustrated with *me* right now?"

"I need you to promise me something," she replied.

"Fine...what?" I sat silently, waiting for her. "Promise you what, Mom?" I prompted impatiently. "Is this about the Lewis family? Do you want me to seriously meet them or something? Like attend some sort of random family reunion?"

"Promise me that you'll never put Gran in a nursing home. That you and Lou will take care of her if anything happens."

Her request was peculiar, even for Mom. "What do you mean? If *what* happens?" I asked.

"Just promise me, Kay."

"You're freaking me out a little, Mom."

"I'm sorry, dear. I was simply thinking today that we hadn't discussed it—a plan for Gran. Oh, that rhymes!" She laughed lightly.

"Um, OK, I promise. Lou and I will find a good nursing home for her, here in New York probably."

"You *won't* put her in a nursing home. You'll take care of her—here in our house."

"Mom, is something wrong? Are you and Dad OK?" My heart started to beat a little faster, and a chill inched up my spine.

"Of course, dear. We're fine. Don't worry about us. I just...wanted to...I hoped you both would have come back for Thanksgiving, so we could talk then. But I wanted to catch up on it today before I...forgot. Where did you spend Thanksgiving, anyway?"

"At Adam's."

"Adam? He's only a passing fancy. I'm not going to worry about him. Say hello to your dad; he's right here."

"Hi, Dad," I said. "Mom hates Adam, doesn't she?"

"Now, Kay, Annette doesn't *hate* anyone. Did she tell you that the new restaurant downtown has one of your paintings?"

"No, she didn't. How'd that happen?"

"Ouch, Annette! Was that one of your secrets? I guess, that's my cue—I better hand the phone back to your mother. Bye, Kay."

"Bye, Dad." I waited a second for Mom to start again. I could hear her say something muffled.

"That father of yours knew very well that the painting downtown was a surprise."

"Which painting? Why didn't you tell me?" I asked.

"When you get home, you can find out. How is it going with the art-studio opening?"

"So far, so good. I'm still working on the layout of the paintings," I explained.

"Of course you are doing *everything* yourself, even though you have an assistant," she said.

"I *can* do it myself! I don't need an assistant; she's only a temp anyway. Are you sure you can't come over to see the studio?" I asked.

"I just…can't be there, Kay," she said. "I'm sorry. I know you're disappointed, but someday you'll understand."

"I get it. It's a long way away, and you don't like the city."

"The city is so noisy I can't hear myself think. I really liked the *Motorcycle Man* series; you should make that the central display. He's *very* kind," she said.

"Kind? He's only a guy in a painting, Mom. Sometimes you can be so strange." I laughed.

She fell quiet again for a few seconds. "Gran is in the greenhouse, and I need to get back out there before she starts pulling up the lemongrass again. I love you, Kay." I could hear her sniffle and take a deep breath.

"I love you too, Mom. Are you sure you're OK?"

"Yes…fine…" She sniffed. "Probably an allergy."

"OK, I'll call you after the opening then and tell you how it went," I promised.

"I'd like that," she said quickly, hanging up the phone. I walked over to the window and watched an ambulance whiz by. When I was a kid, I spent most days outside on the beach or walking in the woods, trapped by stories of the past and desperate for a new start anywhere else. Cape Disappointment and Ilwaco, Washington, felt a world away.

Chinook Wind ✤

The opening was to start in an hour, and I still had to finalize which painting would hang on the main entry wall. Two paintings vied for my attention as I deliberated, straining the patience of my, I guess, *boyfriend*, Adam, an investment banker who tried to appear interested after looking at the same two paintings on and off for the last ten minutes, although he spent much of his time focused on his phone.

Finally, he declared, "I think this is your best one—*Chinook Wind*. This should be the feature, without a doubt. I don't get this other one, anyway; who's the guy with the motorcycle and the dog? Should I be jealous?"

"I told you, he's no one; it was a dream I had that inspired this whole West Coast series. Whoever he is, he's popular. I've sold more of these than any of the others. Since that critic in the *Times* wrote that anyone who sees the *Motorcycle Man* will feel like they've glimpsed a kindred spirit, this guy has been my most requested painting."

"Yeah…I didn't get that part of the review. Don't get me wrong, it's a great painting, but there's something about this guy that I just don't like," Adam complained.

I shook my head, removed the *Motorcycle Man* painting, and hung up *Chinook Wind* again. I stepped back to view it, not yet convinced. Suddenly feeling a chill like ice that caught my breath, I shivered and pulled my sweater tighter to me, crossing my arms for warmth.

"This one reminds me most of you and your...uh...aesthetic. Always fresh and unpredictable," he said, still transfixed by his phone.

"I think those were the exact words your mother used to describe the tofu surprise I brought to Thanksgiving," I replied.

"See! It's all you—fresh, unpredictable, and perfect...*my* Kay."

I smiled, leaning into him for a kiss. "Unpredictable like your beloved stock market—no wonder you like me."

"I don't like you; I *love* you." He looked at me expectantly, waiting for me to return the sentiment. But *something* felt wrong. I couldn't say it, and it had been a week now since he'd dropped the "love" bomb. He'd surprised me by inviting his family over for Thanksgiving so I could meet them. They all piled into his small, designer apartment as if it were a subway during rush hour. When his mom asked if wedding bells were in our future, he smiled broadly, and I crawled out of the window to sit on the fire escape because I couldn't breathe. We'd broken up three times since then, and Thanksgiving was only last week.

"I need more time," I said. He rolled his eyes in protest. "Adam, we only *just* got back together." I thought about Mom calling him a "passing fancy" and wondered what she meant. She was always cryptic and carefree, dropping comments and then making me puzzle over their meaning for months.

He took my hand, looking first disappointed and then concerned. "You're freezing cold! Are you coming down with something?"

"Probably only the stress of today; it's cold in here."

"I hope you're not sick; I *certainly* can't catch something before my presentation next week. I'll pick you up at seven or meet you here?"

"Meet me here; I probably won't have time to go home. There's too much to do." Besides, Adam was never on time.

"OK, *and* I've booked the most exclusive restaurant in New York for dinner," Adam announced.

"Ugh, not another one from that pretentious food guide. The last place had ingredients I couldn't recognize. Exclusive usually means 'trying too hard,'" I complained.

"You'll like this one; it's the best place in Harlem."

"Carota Viola?" I replied eagerly.

"Yes, I know it's your favorite. I had reservations at another restaurant in Manhattan, but Martina was furious when I sent the e-mail invites, and she insisted I change the venue. So Carota Viola is reserved for us starting at eight o'clock; everyone will be there."

"Thanks," I said, thinking Martina knew me well even if Adam didn't—and that I should probably break up with him. Again.

"My pleasure," he said as he checked his phone. "I have to run, Princess. I'll see you soon. And, Kay, don't worry—it's brilliant."

"Thanks." My gaze followed him out the door as the phone rang. I decided to let my assistant handle the call, and I stared at *Chinook Wind* once again, thinking that Adam was wrong. The *Motorcycle Man* painting should be the center of the exhibit; there was something about him that captivated me. All week I'd felt something in the air that my grandmother would describe as "spirits," pulling and pushing me in some direction that I didn't yet understand. The chill struck again so strongly that it forced me to sit down. Suddenly I was feeling as empty and frozen as an ice block.

"Kay!" my assistant yelled from across the studio.

"Alice, what have I said about yelling in the studio? Could you get me some hot tea?" Of course, I realized that, ironically, I was yelling to ask her to *stop* yelling.

She ran over with the phone. "Sorry, boss, but you better take this." Her eyes looked anxious and were filled with pity.

"Hello?" I answered nervously.

"Yes, is this Kay Baker?" a man asked.

"Yes."

"I'm calling from the Astoria Medical Center in Oregon. Your parents were brought in a few minutes ago after a car accident on the highway."

"No! No, that can't be." I leaned into the wall, unable to breathe.

"Henry and Annette Baker of Ilwaco, Washington?" he said, confirming the names of my parents.

"Yes. And my…grandmother?"

"No one else was in the car. We suggest you get here as soon as you can."

"I'll be on the next flight out…I'm in New York, so… um…I'm on my way." I hung up and grabbed my coat and purse. "Alice? Take care of…well…*everything*. I have to go. It's my parents."

At least, after the fact, I thought I'd said something when I'd left. I couldn't remember getting into the taxi for the airport. I left an emergency message for my brother, who was in the navy and at sea. I caught the next flight to Portland, Oregon, and picked up a rental car for what should have been a three-hour drive, but took four hours, due to the darkness and a freak snowstorm to Astoria, Oregon. Just before the plane landed in Portland, I threw up in the bathroom.

My mind kept turning over the conversation with Mom and the promise I'd made to her. I wondered what she'd known and what she hadn't told me. Most importantly, I prayed that they were all right. It had been over ten hours since the phone call, and I couldn't bring myself to call the hospital for an update.

I arrived at the emergency room around two in the morning and found my grandmother, Hannah, sleeping in a chair in the far corner of the waiting area, sitting next to a man who looked like an outdoor clothing catalogue model in his plaid shirt and red down vest. He straightened a blanket across Gran's knees, and I assumed he was a social worker. I stopped short, unsure of what to do next. Gran looked elegant and strong, even at ninety-seven years old, wearing stylish clothes and light makeup with her long white hair carefully braided back, most likely by my mom that morning.

I decided to let her sleep and walked over to the information desk, hoping against hope. A doctor soon appeared with *the* look and asked me to follow him to a nearby room as I remembered Gran telling me about feeling the chill of death, a story that I'd never believed was real. The doctor told me what I already knew: my parents had died, succumbing to the traumatic injuries from the car accident. He was sorry for my loss and let me sit a minute in the room alone, before I went to get Gran and take her home. I cried for a long time. Eventually, I collected myself and stood up to get Gran who was now *my* responsibility. I walked over to her in the waiting area, only to be stopped by the social worker who stood up quickly, stepping in front of Gran like a zealous mall cop.

"Excuse me, that's my grandmother," I said quietly, not wanting to wake her. He stared at me but didn't move. There was something familiar about him, but I was certain that we'd never met. The silence was uncomfortable. "Do you...speak English?" I asked slowly and a little louder, unsure why he was just standing there, staring. He blinked as his face flushed bright red. I didn't know where to look, so I repeated myself. Finally, he nodded. I took a step forward, as did he. "What are you? Some sort of hospital mime?" I suggested in exasperation.

"Uh...sorry...um...she...um...just settled down," he stammered. "They gave her something so she would sleep; please, don't wake her up."

"I wasn't planning on it. Why did they give her a sedative?" I asked, concerned.

"After they told her the news, she reacted...She was inconsolable," he explained evenly.

I sighed. "Why did they even *tell* her? They should have waited for me...Are you a social worker? You can leave now, I'm her granddaughter."

"The neighbor....Sam....*I'm* Sam. I live in the old Tinker house. You must be Kay. I'm so sorry for your loss."

I nodded and sat down next to Gran, bundling my scarf to make a pillow for her as I gently folded some stray hairs back into her braid. I looked over at the neighbor who had crouched down beside me. "Why are you here?" I asked.

"I found Hannah wandering around the neighborhood, lost, and I brought her home. I was going to stay with her until your parents got home, but then we got the call from the hospital. I've been here all night."

"I felt...I should have been here. I could have..."

"Can I drive you home?" he asked. "You'll probably need help with her."

"No. I...uh, I can't just...I..." I couldn't move. I couldn't leave. It took me ten hours traveling like a lunatic, only to learn that they were gone by the time my flight arrived in Portland. And I'd felt it; I'd felt them leave somehow, although that wasn't rational. Could Mom have known? I couldn't think about it, yet it was *all* that I could think about. Had I told them that I loved them? I tried to remember. What had we talked about exactly?

"Can I get you some food or tea or...anything?" he asked.

"No, you've done enough. Thank you. I'm sorry I called you a mime," I said, distracted. "You can go."

"You shouldn't be alone right now. Is there someone else I can call?"

"No. Please...Go."

Outside, snow continued to fall, inch by inch, draping Astoria with an extremely rare white blanket; I knew that we couldn't stay at the hospital, but I also couldn't go home to their house with all their things.

Once the neighbor left, I felt completely alone and lost. A hospital volunteer brought over a blanket and, leaning onto Gran's shoulder, I fell asleep.

Lavender ❃

*S*everal days later, as I stood in Gran's room wearing a new black dress and helping her into hers, I kept reminding myself to breathe. The wind howled outside the windows, and a dark gray sky hung above the incessant snow. We would have to wear boots and change shoes at the church. Everyone kept talking about the impact of extreme temperatures, saying that this was the first snow anyone had seen in the area in decades. Since I'd arrived, the news featured story after story of how people were creatively coping with it, fashioning shovels out of pots and pans or ice scrapers out of compact disc album covers.

"But I don't want to wear my *black* dress to church; it's a depressing color. I want to wear the *red* one," Gran protested, already having forgotten the accident—or at least, it remained temporarily hidden from her in the recesses of her mind.

"I know, but today is a funeral service, so we are wearing black," I said.

"Who died? I hope it wasn't anyone we knew very well," Gran said.

I stared ahead and grabbed the lavender oil, which I would use to help keep Gran calm during the service in case she did remember. Everyone told me it was a bad idea to take her, in her condition, but somewhere in that cloudy brain of mixed memories, she was *still* there. And she would never miss her daughter's funeral. It was worse to tell her again about the accident, and my mother swore that the validation techniques worked best. I dabbed the lavender oil across both our wrists and neck liberally; it would keep us calm during the service, combined with all the chamomile tea I'd plied her with that morning.

"There, I think we're ready. Shall we?" I asked.

"Lavender is lovely. You look very sad."

"Do I?" I feigned a smile. "Let's go; Dorothy's waiting downstairs." Dorothy had lived across the street for as long as I could remember and had been helping my parents a lot with Gran. She was younger than Gran but still well into her eighties, and she had occasionally babysat me and Lou when we were little kids.

At the church, the front row was empty, waiting for us. I insisted on no coffins or pictures, for Gran's sake. There were only the urns from the cremation and flowers; the small church was calmly scented with white lilies. Over a hundred people filled the pews, and I noticed they had added some rows of chairs at the back. We sat in front with Dorothy and Kristin, my friend from high school who still lived in Astoria, about a twenty-minute drive away from Ilwaco and Cape Disappointment. Notably absent were Adam and Lou. Someone put a hand on my shoulder, and I turned, suddenly feeling overwhelmed by the love in the room.

Everyone here loved them. I discovered that the hand on my shoulder belonged to the neighbor I'd met at the hospital. I tried to remember his name as I looked briefly into eyes brimming with sympathy, and I turned back around, overwhelmed and numb. I broke down into tears for the third time that day, and Kristin put her arm around me as Dorothy answered Gran's occasional whispered questions. I focused on breathing, while a storm outside continued to claw at the windows; the wind and hail occasionally drowned out the organ.

After twenty minutes, Kristin touched my hand and leaned over to me. "It's time for you to say something, Kay. Are you OK to do this?"

In my head, I answered no and yes in quick succession. I took another deep breath. The mild sedation of lavender and chamomile allowed me to function; I couldn't cry anymore anyway. I stood up and walked to the lectern, wondering where the last twenty minutes had gone and what I would say.

Once there, I faced the sea of black clothing with the occasional waves of white tissues. Some faces I recognized from school or town; others must have been Mom's patients or Dad's sailing-club friends. They stared. I stared. Another minute of silence passed. The neighbor in the second row coughed. I remembered that his name was Sam…Sam from the hospital. Gran smiled and waved; Dorothy grabbed her hand. I looked down for a few seconds, holding onto the lectern to steady myself. My parents were dead, and I was alone at their funeral. Hail started to tap loudly upon the windows, filling the silent room with a relentless noise as I wondered what Mom and Dad would want me to say.

"Thank you for coming today," I said finally. I stood there for another minute staring blankly, unable to move or say anything else, and was efficiently rescued by Kristin. She gently guided me back to the pew, walking alongside me as the music started and people stood up to sing something about grace. I sat and continued to stare.

After the funeral, I asked Dorothy to take Gran home, while I gathered the strength to represent the family at the reception in one of the church's meeting rooms. Mom would have disapproved of the food spread, which consisted primarily of frosted cupcakes and pies, and Dad would have complained about how cold the meeting hall was. The hall still had remnants of Thanksgiving decorations, with turkeys on the tablecloths, and I suddenly realized that I should have spent more time planning this instead of relying upon the kindness of others.

I stood near the door, where a child's hand-drawn turkey picture was taped to the wall, hugging people whose names I couldn't remember and saying, "Thank you," in response to everything. I didn't have to make sense, but I did have to be there. Most people told me how much they loved them and shared stories about how either Mom or Dad had helped them at one time or another. Eventually I sat down with a glass of wine and a plate of cake that Kristin found for me. I noticed that Sam seemed to be everywhere and nowhere, cleaning dishes in the kitchen, clearing tables of used dishes, or refilling the food so it never ran out. He and Leon, Kristin's husband, managed the reception. "I couldn't have gotten through this without you and Leon." I told Kristin.

"We only want to help."

"Thank you." My eyes drifted toward a void.

"You were right that Hannah should attend, even if she didn't know what was really happening."

Suddenly something about Gran waving at me seemed very funny, and I started to laugh uncontrollably. "She waved at me when I was up at the lectern, like I was at a school play." Tears fell from my eyes as I laughed and cried simultaneously.

Kristin laughed too, handing me another tissue. "Dorothy had to stop her from clapping—could you imagine?" We shared a completely inappropriate laugh as she poured me some more wine.

"I wish Lou were here," I said, serious again.

"I know. I'm sure he does too," Kristin said.

Sam walked by with dishes from the nearby table, asking if he could get us anything. I was starving, and I couldn't remember having eaten anything that morning, but the cake in front of me looked terrible. "Is there any food *without* frosting?" I asked.

He nodded. "I can make you a panini with mozzarella, basil, and tomatoes...no frosting."

"Thank you," I managed to say, feeling rescued again. He patted my shoulder like we were on the same sports team and soon disappeared into the kitchen. How he'd get me a panini from the church kitchen where somehow every appliance was always broken in its own unique way, I had no idea.

"He's a real gem, that Sam," Kristin commented. "He's so helpful. You know what? He reminds me of Leon's brother,

Jackson. Last summer at the family reunion in Alabama, Jackson swooped in and managed to solve any problem that came up. I really thought they'd have to cancel the dance when the power when out, but then, here comes Jackson with a generator for the DJ. I couldn't have married into a nicer family—"

I closed my eyes, unable to focus, and ran my hands through my hair. "What am I going to do?" I whispered distractedly.

"Kay, you will get through this." She reached over and rubbed my shoulder.

"Yes, I will get through this day," I rallied somewhat convincingly as I took a deep breath and changed the subject. "What's the deal with Sam? I mean, where'd he come from? Mom *never* mentioned him, and he's *everywhere* today—and with Gran at the hospital. I don't understand. And he looks so familiar, but I can't place him. Did he go to school with us?" I asked, thinking about his eyes.

"Leon said your Mom talked about him *all* the time at the clinic. Still, a part of me thinks that maybe his being here is less about *them* and more about *you*."

"Please. Maybe I've been in New York too long and forgotten what small town neighbors are like, but I think he's only being nice."

"Our neighbors in Astoria certainly aren't *that* nice."

More strangers walked over to the table to tell me how much they would miss my parents and how my mom had helped their families. I started to cry again. "I'm OK, yes, thank you. Sorry, the tears come in waves." One of them leaned over to hug me. Why did everyone need to touch me? I struggled to breathe.

"Excuse me," Sam said, stepping in. "She hasn't eaten all day; maybe just give her a few minutes?" I didn't know what I appreciated more at that moment: the perfect panini or the fresh air without someone hovering over me.

The strangers nodded and stood up to walk back to their table. Of course all I could say was, "Thank you." He smiled and turned around to pick up some dishes and returned to the kitchen. I took a bite of the sandwich and felt a glimmer of strength return.

New Normal ❀

We were out of everything. The refrigerator looked so empty that people would have assumed we had cleaned it that morning. Unless I could whip up a dinner out of baking soda, an onion, and some herbs from the greenhouse, I would have to leave the house, but the idea of shopping with Gran overwhelmed me. Already this morning she had been in tears about Mom and Dad dying, having remembered it after breakfast, and we'd relived it again. Then we'd spent the rest of the morning with her asking me where her dad was and when he'd be home from work.

Still, we had to eat and that meant shopping for food. I combed my hair, put on some jeans, and otherwise stayed in my favorite Yankees sweatshirt that I had slept in and wore consistently throughout the last two days. I figured that we were going to the grocery store in Ilwaco, not the opera. Still, Gran insisted on getting decked out. She wore the red dress she'd been bugging me about for the last week and then freaked out when we got into the car, spilling the coffee she'd insisted on taking, and we had to start all over again. Two hours later, we were in the car pulling out of the driveway. We drove through town, and I looked out at the water along the harbor of Baker Bay.

Ilwaco is a historic fishing village at the edge of Cape Disappointment, and even today only a thousand or so people live here. Everyone knows *everyone*, not like New York, where no one knows anyone. I missed that anonymity; still the views of the town were unquestionably beautiful, with the faded-brown shingle-sided cottages, the boats in the harbor, and the little chapel.

At the store, Gran insisted on pushing the cart, and of course I had no problem with that—whatever kept her occupied. We started in the produce section, and after I turned my back to grab some grapes, she and the cart were gone. I sighed, took the grapes, and started to track her down. I found her in the dairy section, where she was talking to another shopper about cheese after having placed ten pounds of cheese in the cart. I soon discovered that she was speaking with Scott Wilkes, a high-school classmate of mine.

"Hey, Scott," I said as I lifted all of the cheese out of the cart and returned it to the fridge.

"I heard you were back in town. How's it going, Indian Princess?" he teased, making me roll my eyes.

"Don't be a jerk; you know I don't like being called that. I'm fine. How's Amy?" I asked about his wife, also a former schoolmate and certainly the meanest girl in the county.

"She'll love to see you," Scott began. Then he said loudly across the aisles, "Amy? Hey, you'll never guess who's here."

Gran started to holler out for her now too, thinking it was a game. "Amy? Ammeeee! Amy! Amy..."

Amy appeared from around the aisle, wearing a cashmere sweater set, her hair perfectly in place in long, flowing curls that must have taken her at least an hour to do, even if she did own the local salon. She carried a bag of chocolate chips and set it in the cart.

"Amy? Amy?" Gran continued.

I touched Gran's hand and said, "Good job. You found her! This is Amy."

Gran smiled and Amy looked uncomfortable, although she still took her time looking me over and paying special attention to my sweatshirt that I didn't bother to change regardless of the coffee spill in the car. "Hi, Kay. We heard you dropped out of med school and moved back. All those big-city dreams, and here you are back in Ilwaco."

"I *completed* med school. My parents died," I explained quietly, although of course she knew that already. It was a small town.

"I imagine you must still be very depressed, with your hair like that and wearing…your morning coffee," Amy said, referring to my stained sweatshirt. "It must be hard still being alone without a family, especially at our age."

Scott cringed. He'd always been nicer than Amy, even in school. He interrupted, trying to lighten the conversation. "I expect we'll start hearing about all sorts of unusual things now that you're back in town, Kay. Remember when Gina's hair turned orange after she replaced you on the dance team? Or when a tree fell on Eric's car? Weird stuff tends to happen when you're around, Kay."

Maybe I'd added turmeric to Gina's shampoo, but the tree falling had simply been a thing of nature. I'd hated being teased throughout school as the Indian princess who didn't fit in with anyone else, and Amy had always been the ringleader.

Amy chimed in, "Yes, and I know you had something to do with my hair getting singed by the bonfire at homecoming."

"That was only a gust of wind, Amy. Everyone saw it," I said, defending myself. Mom used to laugh and call me her "coyote," after the trickster in many native stories. I'd never thought much of it and mostly blamed bad luck. Kristin was my only real friend from school, since we were both outcasts who'd banded together. She'd moved to Ilwaco in junior high after the castes had already been set, and the cool girls wouldn't accept her.

Amy continued, "We already warned that neighbor of yours that he should watch out for you." She cackled. "You know, seeing you now I was just thinking how nice it must be not to have to worry about what your hair looks like. Sometimes I get so busy that I think how nice it would be to stay home all day."

I glared at her. Gran tapped my shoulder. "I've got all the cheese for the party. I think ten pounds should be enough," she said efficiently as I looked to see that all the cheese had returned to our cart, plus some. I had no idea what party she thought we were preparing for, and I didn't try to figure it out.

"You're having a cheese party? How...rustic," Amy said derisively. "We're getting ready for little Tommy's Thanksgiving party at school. I'll be baking my famous chocolate-chip cookies, of course. Everyone always says that no event is complete without them," she said, complimenting herself.

She was as petty and rude now as she had been in high school. I missed New York desperately.

"Chocolate-covered purse!" Gran announced, clapping her hands with glee like a small child. "I want one like that, Mom. Can we get one?" she asked me. In her mind she had apparently returned to her childhood. I followed her gaze to find that the chocolate chips in the bag had melted in Amy's cart, and the chocolate had oozed all over her purse.

"What the...my purse! How could that...Come on, Scott. Let's go." She pulled him by the arm while accusing me with her eyes for the mess.

"Well, Kay, I'm sure life will be a lot more interesting here now that our medicine woman has returned," he joked. As they walked away, I could hear him trying to calm Amy down. "I never really liked that purse anyway; let me buy you a new one..."

I looked at the ten pounds of cheese in the cart and decided to ignore it. "Come on, Hannah. Let's finish our shopping before Dad gets home," I said.

"Can we have spaghetti for dinner?" she asked.

"Of course we can, but only if you're a good girl and you help me finish up the shopping really fast," I replied.

"OK, Mom," she agreed, reaching for my hand.

By the time we reached the checkout, we had ten pounds of cheese, five bottles of orange juice, thirty candy bars, six bottles of children's chewable vitamins, ten bottles of pasta sauce, grapes, and a pizza. I had no idea that a woman in her nineties could be so wily in managing to hide things in the cart.

The young checkout girl was someone I didn't recognize, and I was ever so grateful for small favors.

Sam was out in his driveway when we returned, and he walked over to help me unload the groceries from the car. He'd been dropping by the house every day just to check in; we mostly talked about Gran, and he'd always offer to help with something around the house. After helping me unload the groceries in the kitchen and seeing the ridiculous supplies, he brought over a large casserole dish of homemade lasagna and wine later that evening. Aside from Dorothy and Kristin, Sam also became a fixture in my nonexistent "social" life. I described Sam to Martina one day on the phone as my local neighbor-handyman-cook.

Best Two out of Three ✻

At first the big casserole dish of lasagna that Sam brought over annoyed me. I was capable of cooking and didn't need any help, although I burned a pizza because I was cleaning up the converted attic room—now my paint studio—and didn't hear the timer go off. Gran insisted on painting with me and managed to squirt several tubes of oil paint directly onto the wood floor. I had been boxing up the paints so she couldn't get into them again, which I thought took minutes, when the pizza burned. We dined on the most perfect lasagna instead, and I helped myself to two glasses of wine.

The next day I returned the clean lasagna dish to Sam, after saving off the rest in plastic containers in the fridge. I walked next door to his house, after leaving Gran with Dorothy for a while. Sam's house looked similar to ours, probably built at the same time in the 1890s. I heard his dog barking in the backyard as I stepped onto the porch.

Sam answered the door, and straightened the collar on his flannel shirt. "Well, hello, neighbor. This is a nice surprise."

"Thanks for the lasagna. I brought your dish back," I said simply.

"My pleasure…Come in, come in!" He motioned down the entry hall. I hesitated for a second and then walked inside. I followed him to the living room and sat on a cognac brown leather sofa.

"You've done a great job with this place," I observed.

"Thanks. Annette was a big help with the design, actually. She took pity on the bachelor next door and helped me get settled. It was her idea to put the bookcase in the corner. Coffee?"

"Sure, coffee would be great, thanks."

He looked like a professional barista at the big espresso machine in the kitchen, while I looked around at the bookcase. One of the shelves held a framed photo of him out on a boat with some guys who I presumed were his brothers, given the resemblance. Sam returned with two small Americanos and sat on the navy wingback chair across from the sofa.

"Why are you being so nice to me?" I spurted out. "I mean, you barely know me." The second that I said it, I felt like a jerk.

"Someone definitely got acclimated to New York! You're not used to people taking care of you, are you? I get it…the strong and independent type."

"I guess—"

He didn't let me finish. "I spent Thanksgiving with your parents, and for some reason, she pulled out one of the photo albums to show me pictures of you and Louis."

I groaned. "How embarrassing."

"What? You were cute kid," he said. I laughed as he continued. "Anyway, when we were washing the dishes your mom told me that someday I would meet you and you would need help, but be too stubborn to ask for it. 'Help her anyway, Sam,' she told me. 'And make sure she eats something because she's a terrible cook.'"

I rolled my eyes. "Sounds like her," I muttered. "But, *you* don't have to worry about me. I'm fine. I don't need any help."

"She said that you would fight me each step of the way, which so far has turned out to be true. I made a promise that I intend to keep, so you're going to have to just get used to the idea that we're going to be friends."

I sipped the coffee, which was some of the best I'd tasted. I considered that giving Sam a chance was probably in my best interests. "But I don't need any help. I'm fine...We're fine, Gran and I." I repeated, more to convince myself, because I wasn't even on the same continent as 'fine.'

"The lady doth protest too much. You've only proved my point."

I sighed. "You don't know me."

"But I'd like to. Give me a chance, Kay. So, New York, huh? Must be nice to be home, back to a slower pace of life."

"It's only temporary. My brother's going to move up here, and I'll be returning to New York very soon, hopefully. Like any day now, really...I spent my whole life trying to *leave* this town." After a moment, I added, "I don't know why I just said that."

"I used to be a bartender; people confess things to me all the time," he joked.

"Oh, OK." I glanced around the room awkwardly.

"I haven't spent much time in New York. I'm from Baltimore." Sam seemed determined to have a conversation.

"Baltimore, huh?" I offered, shifting in my seat.

"I bet you want to know what brought me here," he said.

"Um…sure, OK. What brought you to Cape Disappointment?" I echoed clumsily.

"The short story is that I'm a chef and I bought the old Sandpiper restaurant on the waterfront. We officially opened last month. I call it Cucina Felice."

"The 'happy kitchen'—that's a good name," I said.

"Thanks, and it is a happy kitchen. It's been a good move for me. You know, I wish you had let me know you needed a caterer for the funeral. Your mom would have hated the food."

"I know," I sighed. "Dorothy insisted on letting her knitting group take care of it. Mom *would* have hated all that frosting and the…cupcakes."

Sam laughed. "She loathed cupcakes."

"Called them a waste of time," I said and laughed. It was nice to talk about Mom with someone whose memory was stable. I relaxed into the comfortable sofa and drank some more coffee.

Sam smiled. "Yes," he said, changing his voice to mimic my mom. "'Either a cake or a muffin, Sam, don't you *dare* have cupcakes at your restaurant.' Annette had very strong opinions on food."

"Why start a restaurant near Cape Disappointment if you're from Baltimore?" I asked.

"My restaurant in Baltimore closed. It wasn't *my* restaurant, but I was head chef. Anyway, the place went bust, and I needed to find something new. I decided to open up my own place and, you know, make a name for myself. At first, I felt drawn to New York City and had a job lined up in Harlem, but…plans changed."

"Harlem! Really? That's where I live. Where in Harlem?"

"Little Italian place, more of a local hole-in-the-wall, really. Probably no place you've heard of: Carota Viola, which in Italian means—"

"The 'purple carrot,' I know. My friend Martina owns it, and my apartment is literally around the corner." I lifted the coffee cup, hoping to camouflage my shock with a long sip.

"Of all the gin joints! So we would have met if I took that job too," Sam said with a mischievous smile. "Hmm…I guess the world moves in mysterious ways, doesn't it? Maybe it's a sign."

"I don't believe in signs," I said quickly.

"Really? But, I certainly do. That's why I came here, after all."

"And what sort of *sign* from the universe brought you to Cape Disappointment?" I asked in disbelief.

"After the New York plan fell through, I felt pretty lost and met my brothers for drinks to try and shake it off. They thought it would be funny if we threw darts at a map to see where I should open up my first restaurant, so we did. I threw a dart and promised to start my restaurant wherever it landed on the map."

"And the dart hit Cape Disappointment. Why didn't you try for best two out of three? I mean, seriously, the name kind of says it all," I replied sarcastically.

Sam laughed. "Yeah, that's exactly what I thought. Why move someplace called 'Cape Disappointment'? I mean, what…Boring, Oregon, or Hell, Michigan, were not appealing options?"

I snickered. "There's a Hell, Michigan?"

"Yes, my brothers found all the unusual city names in the States, trying to convince me not to move here. They eventually gave up though and threw me a great going away party that was baseball themed, and everyone signed an Orioles shirt for me, and we toasted to them someday winning another World Series. Go O's! Wait. Please tell me your time in New York didn't turn you into a Yankees fan."

"It did actually," I said, clearly disappointing him.

"The Yankees! Ouch…I think my heart is breaking. What are the signs of a heart attack anyway? Severe pain…ouch. The *Yankees*? I made lasagna for a Yankees fan? How is it that the world hasn't opened up and swallowed me whole?" he teased dramatically, holding his hand on his chest and faking a stab of pain.

I laughed. "I could have lied to you, but the truth would have come out sooner or later…Why not best two out of three? You seriously moved here because of *one* dart on a map?"

"I'm not *insane*. Of course I did a best two out of three. Followed shortly by the best three out of five. The fifth time I threw the dart with my eyes closed, throwing it backward over my shoulder from across the room," he said, demonstrating with an imaginary dart and his eyes closed.

"And you didn't hit another town that was a better option?"

"That's the thing—I didn't hit another town. *All* the darts ended up in Cape Disappointment."

"You're kidding me. *All* five?" I said. "Come on!"

"It's true! My younger brother even recorded the last two on his phone. I think at least four people watched it later on that video site. Anyway, I figured the universe was trying to tell me something. I mean, what are the odds? This town is barely on the map, and *every* dart…Incredible, right? How can you say that you don't believe in signs after hearing that?" he asked.

"There was probably something magnetic on the wall, or within the stud or something," I replied scientifically. After growing up with stories about destiny and signs, I had insisted upon anchoring my life on reality instead of native legends. "I believe we make our own way in life. Signs and legends are just…fairy tales."

Sam looked unconvinced. "Just because you don't believe in signs, doesn't mean they aren't real."

Meriwether at Sea ❧ December

he next day I spoke with Louis on our weekly phone chat.

"Dad always loved Christmastime the best. He played Santa every year, and I always thought it was amazing how Santa knew my name and also knew *exactly* how naughty I'd been that year. I still can't believe they're gone," my brother said.

"It's dreadful here without you, Lou. I still don't know how I got through that funeral. Thanksgiving is ruined for me, and now the Christmas season…"

"It's not easy for me either."

"I know. At least Gran has no idea that Christmas is around the corner. She keeps complaining about the lazy neighbors leaving their decorations up all year round, instead of waiting for the season like civilized people. We've had an unusually snowy June, in case you were wondering."

Lou laughed, and so did I. It was good to hear. "I don't think we've laughed like that since it happened," he said.

"They loved hearing us laugh. The urns are on the mantle; I didn't know what to do with them. I should bring them to the—"

"We'll take care of the ashes together when I get home." His tone told me that he needed to be a part of this somehow, and that he felt bad about being gone.

"Yes, just you and me." Tears welled up in my eyes, and I took a deep breath. I had to be strong for my little brother. "When are you coming home, anyway?"

"I've been meaning to talk to you about that. Are you going to take Gran with you when you go back to New York?"

"Gran in New York? Don't be absurd! I think we'd lose her all together if I moved her there. She's more stable in the environment she remembers, at least occasionally. Besides, she's ninety-seven years old, for crying out loud."

"So, you're staying in Ilwaco then?"

"What? No, *you're* staying! Getting orders to Cape Disappointment—that's what you said. I'm only here until you…You promised you'd be here by January, February at the latest. We talked about this before the funeral."

"Yeah, but the thing is—"

"Meriwether Louis," I said, angrily using his full name sounding more like a mom than an older sister. I had promised Mom that there would be no nursing home and that Gran would be taken care of at home; still I thought Lou could move home and manage it. And he had agreed.

"What am I supposed to do, Kay? I live on a ship most of the year, and I couldn't take care of her even if I did move. At least you're on terra firma."

"Are you kidding me with this? I have the studio and a *life* in New York!" The arctic wind howled outside the house, and I pulled my sweater closer to me.

"I don't know how to live on land. I'm no good at it. My animal spirit is the whale, remember?"

"You're using an *animal spirit* as an excuse? Seriously? We've never once gone to a tribe meeting or...potlatch... or whatever. You know what I mean," I sighed loudly in frustration.

"You're the oldest and the most responsible. I can barely keep track of my small suitcase, let alone a nearly senile Gran. Besides, you'll have Adam to help out, right?"

"Adam and I broke up two weeks ago; he texted me," I said, realizing how pitiful that sounded.

"I never like any of your boyfriends," Lou said. "And I can't believe that I bothered to learn this one's name. What a jerk!"

I sighed. "Look, Meriwether——" I thought about my promise to mom.

"You and Gran are the only ones who get away with calling me that name."

I took a deep breath. My brother wasn't coming; I was alone, and there was nothing I could do about it. "Fine. Look, I'll figure it out. Just promise you'll come home soon to visit at least. I'm drowning over here, not waving."

"I promise. When we pull into home port, I'll hop on the next plane."

"Yeah, yeah, sure. The *next* plane—I've heard that before. If you don't come home for Christmas, I might disown you," I said.

"Kay, come on. I'll be home for Christmas."

"Don't make promises that you can't keep, Lou." I paused a second to regain my composure. "Gran always said that the spirits would call us home to our Clatsop roots one day."

"Nah, she only said that to *you*. You were always her favorite, the extraordinary *keelalle*, the strongest and most powerful medicine woman in two hundred years. I was only the *boy*—her voice even dropped when she said it."

"*I* don't want to live in Ilwaco, Lou."

"Me neither! You know, Kay, we could put her in a nursing home. There's that nice one in Astoria, and I would help pay for it. You should reconsider it."

I heard someone knocking at the door and knew it had to be Kristin. "*No. No nursing home.* Look, I have to go. Kristin's here. Besides, I'm too mad at you right now to...just...Bye." I hung up the phone and shook my fist at it. I had *no* idea how to make this work.

Kristin patiently listened to my complaints about Louis while she deliberated between Earl Gray and chamomile tea. She had also left Ilwaco after high school, moving to Los Angeles for college, but she'd returned home right after college graduation to take care of her father who had what he called at the time "a touch of cancer." Fortunately, after a lot time in and out of the hospital, he recovered, and Kristin would have moved back to LA if she hadn't fallen in love with one of the doctors, Leon, and they soon married. Now she had two kids, and they all lived happily in Astoria. She felt confident that the same thing would happen to me, and we'd be baby-sitting each other's kids. I, however, had spent most of my life trying to leave Cape Disappointment, and now was no exception.

"I made chamomile. Here," she said, handing me a steaming mug. "You don't need any more caffeine. You and Louis will work this out. Right now I think you've been too cooped up in this house, and what you need is something else to think about. I know! You should ask Sam out on a date, now that you're single again," Kristin suggested.

"Sam and I are just friends. Besides, I'm not interested in dating anyone right now, let alone someone from Ilwaco. Gran takes up most every minute, and I only get a break when Dorothy takes her out for a while. At least she's *here*; my unhelpful brother, on the other hand—"

"Sam lives next door to your house; what could be easier? Handsome, helpful man like that…You're crazy for not asking him out for drinks. I'm pretty sure he's single."

"Adam and I only broke up two weeks ago," I reminded her.

"I never liked him. He was pushy," she said.

"You never *met* him…But he *was* pushy." I felt really cold and grabbed the sweater off my chair; I always kept one handy in this drafty old house. I pulled the sweater on and warmed my hands with the tea cup.

"Whatever, he's out of the picture anyway and I'm glad; you deserve better. Besides, your life is *here* now, whether you like it or not."

"I have my studio and apartment in New York, and friends," I said.

"And how is the studio doing since you left town? Isn't the point of having a studio so that people can meet the artist and see them at work?"

"Things have been…quiet, especially quiet because *this* artist isn't in her studio; she's babysitting her senile grandmother while her brother happily gets on with his life," I said.

Kristin rolled her eyes, unmoved by my grumbling. "And how much does it cost you to keep that apartment that you don't live in? Twenty-five hundred dollars a month? That's my guess for New York rent, at *least*."

"But, it's a *great* location."

"So, *not* living in New York is costing you a fortune! And you're losing money on the studio now too, aren't you?" Kristin said.

"It'll pick up," I replied defensively.

"Kay, what you've done in moving back here isn't easy. Believe me, I get that. I held onto my Los Angeles condo for almost six months after I moved back here. And I would still have it today if a good friend of mine didn't tell it to me like it was. "

"Sure, throw my own advice back in my face—awesome," I said.

"Look, at least close the studio and sublet the apartment. Losing that much money per month is nuts."

"I know you're right, but it's just—"

"Difficult. I get that, but you need to take care of yourself. I'm worried about you."

I still felt chilled, even with the sweater on and my hands warming around a cup of tea—like I had a fever or something. "OK, OK. I'll think about it."

"That's all I ask."

"Let's talk about you. How are you? You look a little tired; are you feeling OK?"

For some reason, I felt that something was wrong. I had an image of her looking jaundiced and holding her back as if she were in pain. It was so real. I looked at her again. No jaundice—she was the picture of health. I could feel it, though, and knew that something wasn't right. Emma called it my "med-sense," because she insisted that I had a sixth sense for medicine although I knew my guesses were just lucky.

"I'm fine, only a little tired. Grady's been sick, and I haven't been able to sleep at all. That kindergarten is like a petri dish. He seems to come home with a different cold every other month."

Suddenly my mind flashed back to reviewing study cards in college. Strangely, the entire deck of cards I imagined had photos of the pancreas. "You aren't in any pain—no back or abdominal pain or anything like that?"

"What are you talking about? No, nothing, I'm fine. I'm a doctor's wife; Leon would know if something was wrong. You're being weird and trying to change the subject."

Something was wrong, though. At med school they often told us that if we heard hoofbeats, we should think "horses," not "zebras"—it's better to assume the more typical diagnosis, not the exotic and rare worst-case scenarios. I suddenly felt convinced that Kristin had pancreatic cancer. Forgetting the zebras, I skipped straight to unicorns: It was absurd to think that over a cup of tea I could sense an otherwise un-diagnosable cancer, yet *everything* in my mind told me I was correct. If it was nothing, then a test would confirm it, but if I was right…I hoped I wasn't right, but my med-sense *knew* I was. "Listen, this is going to sound crazy, but I think you need to see some-one and get some labs run on your pancreas. And a CT. Leon can prescribe them."

"You're right; it does sound insane. You're scaring me, Kay. You look like Leon did when he told me about Dad's cancer."

I reached for her hand and feigned a reassuring smile that I'd learned watching the senior osteopaths in the clinic. "It's probably nothing, and if so, the test will confirm it. Probably all this stuff from Gran going to my head—you know, the 'great prophecy.' Still, I really want you to get tested—like, this week." I smiled again, trying to reassure her.

Kristin eyed me suspiciously. "Your mom was right about my dad's diagnosis, weeks before Leon could confirm it. He said she had a sort of sixth sense for diagnosing people. Still… Look, I'll make you a deal. You close the studio and sublet your apartment, and I'll get tested."

All I could think of was protecting my friend. I sensed her cancer; I could practically smell it. It was the eeriest feeling, and ludicrous. Years with osteopaths and clinics, and never had my med-sense alerted me so intensely. I would have done any-thing in that moment to get her to agree, and closing my studio then seemed like a minor detail. "Done," I said. "I'll call today and make the arrangements."

"Wow, you are serious…um…OK, I'll talk to Leon and get something set up. You're kind of freaking me out now."

"You and me both. My life is suddenly so very small, locked in this house with Gran, trying to keep her from burning the place down. Maybe I'm catching her dementia, and now I'm a little off too."

Kristin smiled. "Newsflash: you were always a little bit off, oh powerful medicine woman."

I laughed. "Thanks, I needed that."

Christmas ❁

Our house was the only one on the block without Christmas lights. We got a tree only because Dorothy insisted and paid some teenager to deliver it to the house. She stood in the living room, supervising the tree installation.

"It's too bad that Sam went back East for the holidays; otherwise, he could have put the lights on the house for you," she commented. "You should have asked him."

Sam had volunteered to put up the lights before he'd left. However, I'd declined and explained that it would be too confusing for Gran. He understood and let it be. We saw each other all the time, and he often came over with dinner to-go from his restaurant, pretending he needed our opinions on the recipes. Of course, I knew that he was simply honoring his promise to mom. Since he was a terrific chef, I also came to the conclusion that I'd be an idiot to refuse.

Gran smiled. "Sam's a dog spirit, Kehlok, and you should meet him. He's so handsome! Why is this boy putting a tree in the living room?"

"Tomorrow is Christmas Day, Gran," I said, answering the question for the third time in the last twenty minutes.

"Is it really?"

"Yes, *still*." I sighed, starting to lose my patience. "Thanks, Dorothy. I do appreciate the tree and the thought. We'll have fun decorating it, right, Gran?" I simply wanted Dorothy and the teenager to leave. Christmas without my parents, and most likely without my brother, spent answering questions from Gran about why we had a Christmas tree in the living room— it was all a bit much for me.

"Don't tell Louis, but we got him a tricycle this year. A lovely red one!" Gran exclaimed, delighted.

Louis *had* gotten a tricycle for Christmas over twenty years ago. I forced a smile as the boy finished with the tree. I tipped him five dollars and sent him on his way. Dorothy followed him out, mentioning that Gran looked a little tired. After closing the door behind them, I returned to the living room to decorate the tree with Gran. She had opened one of the ornament boxes and was inspecting the contents.

"Should we wait for your mother to get home or decorate the tree ourselves as a surprise?" she asked.

"Let's surprise her and decorate it now," I said conspiratorially, pained with knowing that Mom was never coming home.

She grinned and then froze as her expression changed quickly; maybe she'd seen the pain flash across my eyes at the mention of Mom. "I feel like I'm forgetting something important," she said. "It's something very sad."

I put my hand on her shoulder. "Should we start with the lights?" No need for her to lose Mom again right now. She had remembered the night before and cried for hours. I'd left everything in their bedroom the same, so when she walked by it, nothing was out of place. Gran and I endured constant time travel inside this museum; the less things changed, the better. That's why I didn't want a Christmas tree or lights on the house.

At breakfast the next day, Gran seemed to be very present, and she didn't even ask why there was snow on the ground in June. I considered that maybe the morning vitamin shakes I made her did help. This time I tried a combination of kale, apples, beetroot, and cherries.

"What's this?" she asked.

"Some new medicine that I'm working on; it should help with your memory," I replied. She drank it, and I could tell that my recipes were at least becoming more palatable. Luckily all her years of dancing and staying active meant that, aside from the dementia, Gran was in terrific shape. I watched her closely, making sure she drank all of it. I'd made waffles that morning as a special breakfast; it was Christmas after all.

"Annette always makes waffles on Christmas Day, and there's a tree in the living room," she said and glanced over, piecing together the clues. "Is it Christmas Day, Kehlok?"

"Yes, it is. Merry Christmas, Gran," I said, walking over to give her a hug. "I love you."

"Merry Christmas, my dear girl. I am so grateful that you've come home to stay with me. This is the first Christmas without them, right?" she asked hesitantly, unsure of her own grip on the facts.

"Yes, that's right."

"We must carry on with love and light—no tears today." I held on too tightly as tears rolled down my cheek, regardless.

For this moment, I was not alone; I had my grandmother back. I couldn't have asked for anything else for Christmas.

Pushing my tears gently away, Gran looked at me closely. "Don't cry, my dear coyote girl; don't cry. Let's finish our breakfast, and let me tell you the story of how Tamahna met Lewis. It is the greatest love story *never* told." I smiled as Gran remembered our Christmas-morning tradition. She told this story every year. I'd been hoping she would tell it today if she knew it was Christmas.

"Wait, let me get the video camera," I said hurriedly. I'd taken to recording her on her good days when she told me the stories I would have wanted her or Mom to tell my children someday. "Why don't we do it now and eat after?" I suggested, knowing that she might be in another time and place by the time we finished breakfast.

"OK. In that case, let me get gorgeous first." Gran added a touch of lipstick while I set the camera on the tripod near the sofa. "How do I look?"

"Very glamorous," I replied supportively. These lucid moments were becoming rare, so I wasted no time. "OK, whenever you're ready, it's recording now."

"Hello, my future darling great-grandchildren; this is your great-grandmother, Hannah, talking to you on Christmas Day, a day of more than one miracle. I will tell you the story of Tamahna and Lewis, who met on Christmas Day, which is the start of the greatest love story *never* told. Kay, come over here and sit by me; you start."

I followed her direction, and she placed her hand on my knee. This was a story I knew very well, as Gran and Mom had often also used it as a bedtime story when I was little. "OK, so, it was on Christmas Day in 1805 when Captains Meriwether Lewis and William Clark and their corps had almost completed building Fort Clatsop. To celebrate the day, they fired a few rounds of ammunition thundering into the air and Meriwether gave everyone an extra ration of tobacco."

Gran interrupted, "That's right, dear girl; it was otherwise a rather unremarkable day at Fort Clatsop, where the men worked on completing the chimneys for their huts, and some were preparing a Christmas dinner of boiled elk meat and duck potatoes, known locally as wapato roots. The gunshots signaled the Clatsop chief that it was time to visit the camp. He had been watching the men building for a few weeks now, without going over to meet them. His braves reported that they had seen a baby, a Shoshoni woman, and a large black dog that looked like a small horse. The keealle, the tribe's medicine woman, said they must wait for the thunder before visiting the white chiefs. That day, the thunder of gunshots provided the signal to approach. Now, Kay, you tell them about Chief Conoway and his keealle."

I chimed in, "*Tyee* Conoway introduced himself through his translator, a young man from the Tillamook tribe who had learned English from sailors and spoke Chinook jargon like the Clatsop. The Shoshoni woman, Sacajawea, introduced Tyee Long Knife, pointing to Meriwether Lewis, and Red Hair, obviously William Clark. Everyone knew that Lewis was the chief, and he led the discussion with Conoway. Chief Conoway told Long Knife and Red Hair that his village was seven miles away, where two hundred people lived. Familiar with white men traders and sailors, like Sea Captain Robert Gray, the chief brought fishhooks and tobacco as gifts to these foreigners who were building a home within his lands. After the gifts were exchanged, the tribe's powerful keelalle, Tamahna, arrived on horseback from the east, surprising all the men except for the Chief, who seemed to know exactly when she would arrive."

Gran added, "You remember it well, child. I find myself forgetting *some* of the details, but I can tell you all about Tamahna, who's Christian name was Anna, the last of the most powerful keelalles. Anna spoke English, but she let the translator speak for them while she surveyed the white chiefs. She leapt off her horse effortlessly like an acrobat, walking gracefully yet fearlessly like a warrior. Lewis stood speechless, astounded by her beauty. The interpreter explained in Chinook jargon, 'Anna mamook tamahnous.' Anna stared at Meriwether, seeming not to believe her own eyes. When the interpreter and Clark started to discuss the fishhooks and other items, she silenced them with a flick of her hand. And she said…she said…Oh, it's right at the tip of my tongue. Kay, do you remember exactly what she said?" Gran looked over at me.

I nodded. "Yes, I do. She said, 'I am sorry that I could not be here when you arrived. Our Nehalem brothers fell ill with smallpox and I had to help their village.'"

Gran nodded and I could see her eyes twinkle as she remembered the story, reminding me of how she used to act it out for me with hand gestures and different voices when I was little. When asked in elementary school who my favorite actress was, I told people it was my Gran.

"Yes, that's right! Oh, and then Meriwether stared, lost for words—it was love at first sight. Clark smiled, elbowing his friend to wake him up from his trance, having never seen Meriwether so taken by any woman in his life. None of the teenage southern debutantes thrown into Lewis's path held a candle to Tamahna. Clark had never seen Lewis at a loss for words, not once. 'How many died?' Lewis asked when he had finally managed the courage to speak. Tamahna looked at him curiously. 'None.' Chief Conoway smiled proudly and said that his keelalle was the most powerful in the land. Clark then thanked the chief for providing food when they were trapped in the 'Dismal Nitch.' The chief replied that it was the keelalle's wish. Then Tamahna stepped forward and reached for Lewis's hand and she said...she said..."

I touched her hand. "Tamahna said, 'You are the Boston-man with no ship—the man who walked across the world with the red-haired brave and a black dog. Where is the dog?' she asked, wanting to see proof with her own eyes that her vision was real."

Gran smiled and continued, "Yes, I remember now. Then Tyee Long Knife whistled for his dog, and the Newfoundland bounded over to him. He said, 'This is Seaman, my dog.' Tyee Conoway looked knowingly at his keelalle, and she acknowledged him with a nod, confirming her vision was true. She then looked at Tyee Long Knife and said...and said..." Gran paused as a dark shadow crossed her eyes. She stood up. "I think that's enough for today, Kay; I'm feeling a little tired. I think I will nap for a bit," she said, starting down the hallway.

"What about breakfast?" I asked, reaching over to shut the camera off.

"But we just ate lunch, silly. That meatloaf of your mother's is too heavy for me. I'm going to take a nap," she insisted. And she was gone again, lost in her own mind.

I grabbed a waffle from the kitchen island and returned to the sofa. I picked up where Gran left off, not caring that no one was there except for mom and dad's urns on the mantle to hear me. "Tamahna said, 'I have been waiting for you my whole life.' We tell this story so that our family will remember through the generations, as the Clatsop have always done."

After watching the end of an old black-and-white movie on TV as I finished my coffee, I went out to the greenhouse to see if there were some herb combinations I could try to use in the shakes I made for Gran. Today's shake had seemed to be successful, at least for a little while, so I planned to try the same recipe again. She didn't mind the gingko, but she couldn't stand the taste of the ginseng. I walked around the greenhouse, cutting some more gingko leaves, and I noticed a turmeric plant in the corner by the lemongrass. I cut a few leaves of turmeric as well and returned to the kitchen. Perhaps I could add the turmeric to something for dinner tonight. Sam had left us what he called "Christmas rigatoni," along with some vegetable soup, and I figured the turmeric in the soup would be a good addition, knowing it would help Gran's memory.

I decided to check my e-mail. The studio had closed a few days ago, and everything was packed up in storage, along with my apartment. The new renter would move in after New Year's Day on a new lease, and both my realtor and property manager congratulated themselves on how quickly they were able to finish everything. With a few e-mails and phone calls, New York was no longer my home; everything I had was either here in the house or boxed up in a New Jersey storage unit.

Mint and Lemon ✤ January

*N*ew Year's Day, I woke to a blaring noise that could have been a rocket launch. I threw on a robe and stumbled down the stairs, making my way toward the noise. Throwing open the door, I stormed over toward the ingrate on the motorcycle along a path between snow banks that someone else had already shoveled.

"Do you have *any idea* what time it is?" I asked.

The sound stopped suddenly, as Sam looked over. "Yeah, sure. Do you?" he asked, looking me over as I stood there angrily in my pajamas and robe.

I glared. "Sam! It's the crack of dawn, and you're out here with your dog barking and motorcycle…revving!"

"Actually, it's the crack of *noon* on a Saturday. Boy, you're sure grumpy when you wake up. Happy New Year, by the way."

"What? I don't believe it."

"I'm only being honest. You're a grump. And thanks for *not* asking. Yes, I had a good trip to Baltimore and got back last night. It's good to see you too," he said.

"I'm sorry…It's nice to see you, and I'm glad you had a good trip home. I meant that I didn't *believe* it was *noon*. Sorry. I don't mean to be a jerk. I've maybe gotten a whole five hours in the last three days. Gran——" Pausing for a second, I lost my train of thought.

"It's noon, Kay. Here, look at my watch," he said, moving his arm toward me. I reached for his arm to see the time more closely, and the second I did, his Labrador retriever jumped up and latched onto my hand. I smacked it back, and the dog growled but then sat quietly next to Sam as if nothing had happened.

"Your dog *bit* me!" Icy wind blew through the neighborhood, and the snow began to fall. I realized my fleece robe was hardly suitable for outdoor wear.

Sam picked up the dog in his arms. "Oh my gosh! I'm so sorry about that. Neb has *never* bitten anyone before. You're bleeding. Come inside and let me clean that up for you. That looks awful." I looked over to my house, worried about Gran waking up alone. "We can go over to your house, sure," he said. "Let me put this rascal in my house first." Swiftly he ushered the dog into his house along with a "bad dog" and then was right behind me as I opened the door.

I sat down at the kitchen island. "I can't believe this!"

"You don't happen to have any penicillin or antibiotics around the house, do you?" he asked after handing me a wad of paper towels to catch the blood.

"Not in *this* house."

"Why not?"

"My family doesn't believe in 'modern' medicine," I said.

"Oh really? What about UFOs or the moon landing… What? You started it," he said, grumbling under his breath.

I rolled my eyes and disregarded the comment. "There should be a bottle of witch hazel in the cabinet above the sink."

"Witch hazel? Um, OK, this one in the yellow bottle that looks like it was last filled in 1801 by an apothecary?"

"Yes, that's the one. And next can you go out to the greenhouse and grab me a marigold—actually two."

"Marigolds?"

"You don't know what a marigold looks like?"

"Of course I do," he said, annoyed.

"Terrific," I said sarcastically. "They should be easy to find—probably planted near the tomatoes. And a handful of mint too." I watched him walk out the patio door and stood up to find the mortar and pestle in the cupboard by the refrigerator. He returned shortly, holding two marigolds and a handful of lemon balm and looking at me as if I were crazy.

"This isn't mint, but it was by the tomatoes and kind of looks like mint, so I grabbed it," he said.

"Thanks. It's lemon balm, part of the same family. It's easy to confuse them, but I figured you'd find it if I asked for mint. Imagine—using *mint* for a dog bite!" I chuckled at the absurdity.

Sam continued looking at me like I had snapped. "Right… Please let me call a Doctor. Someone should look at this. You probably need a tetanus shot at least."

I shook my head, took the marigolds and started mashing them up with the mortar and pestle; then I added in the lemon balm. Once they were mashed finely, I added a few drops of witch hazel and some beeswax to make a paste. I moved to the sink and poured some witch hazel straight onto the bitten area, quickly making a face at the stinging sensation. Sitting down again, I asked Sam to smooth the salve onto my hand.

"Don't worry about this," I said. "It's no big deal, really. I'm sure you've trained Cujo better."

"You want me to put this flower mash on the dog bite? Let me just take you to the clinic in Astoria," he protested.

I sighed. "Oh please, this is *nothing*. I don't need a doctor or a tetanus shot. Come on, I'm left-handed, and I won't be able to layer it on evenly, so yes, I need your help. Use the spatula there and smooth some over it, gently."

"What was the witch hazel for?" he asked.

"It'll clean the wound."

"And the marigold and lemon balm mash?"

"Nature's antibiotics, for cuts and bites anyway," I told him.

"Where'd you learn all this?"

"I…uh, come from a *long* line of…*alternative*-medicine providers. Besides, I'm a doctor…well, almost. I haven't done a residency or the exams yet."

"Oh, right. You're the medicine woman from New York City. How could I forget?" he asked.

"Hand me that cheesecloth and wrap it around my hand. Tie it with a bow, not too tight."

"I was a Boy Scout; I know how to tie a knot. You didn't answer my question."

"You didn't ask a question. You know, your motorcycle is *really* loud, and your dog was barking *all* morning," I said. I stood up, now that the dog bite was taken care of, and started making a pot of coffee. I thought about the motorcycle and the Labrador. I studied Sam's face, wondering if it was possible, as I likewise reminded myself that I didn't believe in signs.

"Actually, you probably heard the snowblower. I cleared your sidewalks and driveway this morning before I pulled the bike out. Neb gets freaked out by the snowblower, and she barks at it. I figured you didn't have time to shovel, and I don't mind. Must be a guy thing—you know, big machines," Sam told me.

Now I sounded mean and ungrateful. I wondered why Mom hadn't told me about him. I bet she'd seen him coming. "I'm just...well...um...never mind. Do you want some coffee?" I didn't know what to say about anything. Mom always seemed to know what would happen next and I wished she were here.

"Sure, thanks. So you just woke up?"

"I didn't sleep well. Gran woke me up at two, three, four, and five, asking about buying more bat traps, whatever those are. And then my brother called at six. I thought after his call that I'd only been asleep for an hour."

"She means spider traps. You can get them from the hardware store."

"Spider traps?" I asked.

"Yeah, those paper tents with double-stick tape stuff inside them to catch the spiders," Sam explained.

"Why did she call them 'bat traps'?"

"Didn't they tell you? Your mom found a bat in one of them about a month ago, when they came back from vacation. The thing must have flown into it and gotten stuck."

"Eeew."

"Hannah told me all about it—several times. It was the story of the neighborhood for at least two weeks."

"Yeah, she can be...*repetitive*. But I think it helps her, especially when she remembers something. Thanks. I'll get some today."

We heard Gran's feet on the stairs, and she soon entered the kitchen.

"Kehlok, you're home from school early! Who's your friend?"

"This is Sam," I said. Upon seeing him, her eyes refocused and I could tell she had remembered who he was.

"Of course...Yes. I know that. I remember that, of course. Hello, Sam. Kay, what happened to your arm?"

"Sam's dog bit me."

Gran looked concerned. "That's very bad, Kay. A dog is a loyal spirit. A bite is a sign that your spirit is out of balance, and you need to pay attention to something that you are refusing to accept."

Sam joined in. "Neb's never bitten anyone before, not ever—must be something about *you*."

"Seriously, you're blaming *me* for this?" I said, raising my hand to show him the cheesecloth bandage.

"I'm merely agreeing with your grandmother," Sam said, defending his comment.

"What kind of name is Neb for a dog?" I asked to change the subject.

"It's short for *nebbia*, which is Italian for 'fog.' I found her out by the lighthouse on a foggy morning, on my first walk up there just after I moved here. I had no idea until I moved here that the Cape Disappointment lighthouse is the oldest functioning lighthouse on the West Coast or that it would be surrounded by cannons from the Civil War. Anyway, it was weird: when I got to the lighthouse, I saw Neb, and she ran up to me like she belonged to me. She's been with me ever since," Sam explained.

"Finding your animal spirit at the *veil*, now that is remarkable, Sam!" Gran exclaimed. "The veil is a magical place where our world touches the spirit world. It's why generations of our family have lived here, at the end of the world, as Tamahna called it."

I shifted in my seat nervously. Gran would never have said that to anyone outside of the family.

Sam seemed to sense my discomfort and continued on without missing a beat. "Anyway, Neb followed me home and has been with me ever since. I put up tons of flyers and asked around with the local vets, but no one ever claimed her. I guess it was meant to be...just another sign. My spirit is obviously not out of balance, because Neb's never bitten me," Sam joked.

"*I'm* not out of balance, just sleep deprived. And there are no such things as signs. Neb probably smelled food which is why she followed you," I protested.

Gran looked at me suspiciously, already forgetting her sleeplessness. "Of course there are signs, all around us, every day! Here, let me see that." She took my hand and untied the cheesecloth to inspect my work.

"Well?" I asked, seeking her approval while disregarding her comment on signs.

"Fresh marigold...and is that lemon balm? Why didn't you use the dried marigold in the pantry? Why add the lemon balm?"

I didn't know; I suddenly remembered that dried marigold was what should have been used, and never had I seen lemon balm used for an animal bite. "I'm not sure. I must have forgotten."

She smiled. "Let's see how it looks tomorrow, Kehlok. I think you are starting to come into your own. I'm going to get Annette. Your mother must see this. She'll be so happy to see you working in medicine."

"Mom's out...shopping," I said as evenly as possible, using the validation techniques the doctors told us about for Alzheimer's patients.

"Shopping?" Gran exclaimed. "Why didn't she go when you were at school? Your father will be home soon for dinner, and she will be late, Kehlok."

I stared at her. How cruel it was to be alone in grief and loss, yet not alone. To pretend every day that they were alive and just around the corner, while being with someone who was both there and simultaneously gone.

Sam interrupted with a welcome distraction. "What does *Kehlok* mean, Hannah?"

"It's her name, silly! She's the namesake of her great-great-great-grandmother Kehlok who was born in 1806. It's Chinook jargon for 'swan.' Swans can see the future and heal others by transforming natural elements. They are the most ancient totem and the most powerful. Kehlok is destined to

66

be the most powerful medicine woman in two centuries: the tenth first-born girl of ten generations of keelalles."

"Glad you asked, huh?" I asked Sam. There was no chance of putting that back in the box now. At least in New York, I was so far away I could pretend to have an average life and an ordinary family.

"I suppose that I'll start dinner then; how about a fish fry?" Gran said purposefully, taking a skillet from off its hook.

"Let *me* cook today, Gran," I said quickly, standing up to take the pan away from her. Last time she'd tried to cook, she'd set the kitchen curtains on fire. "We're learning about the first Thanksgiving in school, and I need to make mashed potatoes for my homework. Sam was just leaving anyway."

"Yes, I was," Sam agreed. I walked him to the door. He noticed a yellow note taped on the door and read it out loud. "'Don't go outside without telling Kehlok'?" He titled his head. "Hannah's a bit of flight risk, isn't she?"

"Yes. Yesterday she decided to walk around the neighborhood in only her pajamas and got lost, poor thing. Took me twenty minutes to find her, and she was nearly hypothermic by the time I did."

"Hey, are you OK?" he whispered, motioning toward Gran.

"Fine, everything is fine," I lied.

"Again, I'm sorry about Neb. Promise me that you'll see a doctor."

Pots clanged in the kitchen, and I turned nervously, worried about what Gran was up to. "I have to...be with her."

Sam raised his eyebrow. "I'm fine. Really," I replied, closing the door on him and the world. When I returned to the kitchen, Gran held a pan in her hand and looked up at me, confused.

"I can't remember why I got this out," she said. "I feel like I'm forgetting something."

I took the pan from her and put it away. "It's OK, Gran. We all forget things sometimes. Sit down and I'll make you a cup of tea."

"I feel like I'm forgetting something really *important*. Well...never mind. I suppose it's only my age. Oh, and I didn't like that weird breakfast shake you gave me, Kay. What was that anyway? Carrots, apples, and?"

"Winter cherry," I replied. I'd read it was helpful for Alzheimer's patients, but it didn't seem to have any effect on her. The beetroot shakes seemed to help her for a while over Christmas, but now she'd slide into dementia more frequently and nothing seemed to work.

"I didn't like it."

"Noted, Gran. Do you remember where the journals are? You know, the Meriwether Lewis journals?" I asked her hopefully. I asked her this question every now and then, hoping that one time she'd remember.

"Your mom should be home soon, dear. Why don't you ask her?"

Our family stories said that Meriwether Lewis made another complete copy of his journals while wintering at Fort Clatsop and that he gave one copy to his wife, my four-times great-grandmother Tamahna, for safekeeping in case anything happened to him on the journey home. They'd been passed down through the generations, and I didn't know where they were. Mom and Gran did, but now Mom was gone...and so was Gran.

The Letter ❋

*K*ristin dropped by the next day with some startling news. She had gotten the medical tests, and they all came back with cancer markers. Doctors had already scheduled her for a surgery this week; everything was moving really fast once they discovered it and determined it was operable.

"I can't tell you how grateful I am to you, Kay," Kristin said. "Leon and the doctors all said that it's a miracle catch. It's rare to ever find pancreatic cancer when it's still *operable* because most patients don't see anyone until the pain hits them. By that point, it's usually inoperable and too late. Horrible disease. You're my angel, and I have no idea how you did it. How did you know?"

"Lucky guess." I honestly had no idea.

"But there weren't *any* symptoms. My own husband, a cancer specialist, didn't see anything until that test."

"What's important here is that you're going to be OK. Let's focus on that. Oh, and you'll be delighted to know that I have closed the studio and sublet my apartment too. All my paintings and everything else are boxed up in a New Jersey storage unit. So that's progress, right?" I said.

"Will wonders never cease?" There was a knock at the door, and I looked at Kristin. "Expecting someone? Like a handsome neighbor, maybe? I hear you two are together all the time these days," she said.

"I'm not expecting anyone. You know Sam and I are just friends," I said, a little annoyed as I walked to the door. Sam stood on the porch with a bag full of "bat traps" from the hardware store. I had completely forgotten to get them, and I couldn't imagine the nightmare of possibly losing Gran in the hardware store with all the saws and tools.

"Thanks. I almost forgot about these. I'm surprised you came back after all the weirdness yesterday," I said, opening the door. He looked ruggedly handsome. His face definitely reminded me of someone...those cheekbones that I spent weeks painting to get the shadow exactly right and the slight curve of his eyebrow when he smiled. But how was that possible? Mom used to say that coyote spirits only saw things when they were ready and that someday I would believe in signs and legends.

"No problem. I also wanted to check on your hand and see how the patient was doing," he said, concerned.

I glanced down nervously, wanting him to leave yet desperately hoping he would stay. I wished that I wasn't wearing a stupid T-shirt and velour sweatpants. It felt like I was under a spell. The silence was soon broken by Kristin, who had come over to the door already wearing her coat once she saw who it was.

"Oh, look, the *handsome neighbor* is here, Kay. Hi, Sam. How nice to see you again. Why don't you come in for a coffee?

Dorothy took Hannah to church with her, so Kay has a break and time to herself. Besides, I have to rush home," Kristin explained quickly.

"Coffee would be great. Thanks," Sam replied, stepping inside.

"Terrific," Kristin said, pushing her way out the door as if the house were on fire. "Leon texted me, and I need to get back early, evidently...a macaroni-and-cheese emergency. See you two later, and I'll let you know the plans for this week. Oh, and thanks again, angel-girl."

"Kristin," I hollered, but she ignored me and was quickly in her car, pulling out of the driveway. I closed the door and met Sam, who was already in the kitchen, pouring himself a cup of coffee with a Cheshire-cat smile.

"So, I'm the handsome neighbor, huh?" he said proudly. "And what the heck is a macaroni-and-cheese emergency?"

"She...uh...well, that's how...she's just..." I rambled. Finally recognizing Sam as the motorcycle man from my paintings had left me stunned.

"That's OK. I'm quite happy to be known as the *handsome* neighbor," he said smugly.

"There's not really much competition in the neighborhood when you think about it, given the other options are Dorothy, who's in her eighties, and then Mr. Burdock, who's got the lazy eye. So, enjoy the trophy, I guess." I was painfully aware how silly I sounded.

Sam laughed. "And there's a *trophy*? Even better. But enough about me and my handsomeness. I also came over to check on your hand after the bite from Neb yesterday. Did you get that tetanus shot?"

"No."

"Uh-oh, no modern medicine? You know that you need a shot, right?"

"Take a look for yourself," I said, reaching my hand out toward him. He held my wrist, and I caught my breath.

"Where's the bite?" he asked.

"I honestly have no idea. I took the cheesecloth off before taking a shower this morning, and it's gone. It did happen, right? I mean, you were there, and you *saw* it. I'm starting to think I imagined the whole thing."

"That's—"

"Impossible, right? I mean, yesterday there were teeth marks in my hand after Neb went all *Cujo* on me, and today...nothing." I'd never taken the keelalle stories seriously, and now suddenly, at least a part of me had to acknowledge that they *might* be true—that this might be, for lack of a better word, magic.

"What did Hannah say?" Sam asked.

"She said that dog has never bitten anyone and that it's wrong to make up stories," I replied.

"So she blanked it," Sam said.

The phone rang. "*Totally* blanked it. Sorry, I have to get this. It's my storage company in Jersey; my payment was returned for some reason and I've been trying to get them on the phone all morning, but we keep playing phone tag."

"Hello? Is this Kay Baker?" the woman on the phone asked.

"Yes."

"I'm very sorry, ma'am, but we had a fire last night due to an electrical fault."

"At the storage building?" My stomach fell.

"Yes. The good news is that not all of the units were damaged in the fire, but we have to notify all the renters regardless," she explained mechanically, as if this was the hundredth time she'd said those words today.

"Oh, so my things are OK?" I felt relieved.

"No, ma'am, unfortunately your unit was very close to the fire, and everything was destroyed. We've returned your payment and will send you a form for your insurance company."

"*Everything?*" I asked, shocked.

"I'm very sorry, ma'am. We'll send you all the information in the mail as soon as possible." I hung up and sat down on the kitchen floor.

"What happened?" Sam asked, concerned, as he rushed to sit down next to me.

"Everything is…gone. My things were all in storage in Jersey, and there was a fire. *Everything* was destroyed."

"I'm sorry, Kay," he said, putting his hand on my knee.

"I've lost my parents, my studio, my apartment, and now everything else in a matter of weeks. *Years* of my life just… erased. Everything I worked toward, everything *real*. Now all I have is a senile grandmother and an old, drafty house by Cape Disappointment. My life is a surreal disaster." I didn't mention that I'd also starting wondering whether there was some truth to the legends I grew up with.

"They are just things, and things can be replaced. I'm just glad that you're OK. Think of it as a sign of a fresh start."

I wiped tears from my eyes, and sighed. "Not again with the signs," I grumbled.

"I happen to believe in them, even if you don't. How else do you explain this?" Sam asked, as he reached into his pocket for his wallet and pulled out a worn envelope. "Annette gave me something for you at Thanksgiving—a letter."

"What? Mom gave you a letter for me? Why didn't you give it to me before? It's been almost two *months* since the funeral!"

"She gave me strict instructions that I was only to give you this the day after the dog bite. It didn't make any sense, and I'd been thinking about giving it to you for a long time. But she was so serious that any time I thought of it, I'd hear her voice in my head: 'Wait until the day after the dog bite…that will be your sign.'"

I pulled the envelope toward me and quickly opened it, my hands shaking.

Sam stood up and held out his hand to pull me up. "Sit down at the table and read the letter. I'll make some breakfast."

"Thank you," I managed to say, standing up from the floor to sit at the kitchen island.

My dearest daughter,

There are so many things I wanted to tell you, but there is not much time left for me. I love you and Louis so very much.

Find John Lane on the tribal council in Seaside, Oregon, and he can help you learn the old ways and the things I am not there to teach you.

I asked Sam to give you this letter today, a day you would feel most alone. Our power is derived from love, and a keelalle's soul mate is drawn to her before they even meet. Not believing in the signs doesn't make them any less real.

The world needs a powerful healer. Embrace your destiny, for you are powerful beyond measure.

Love always,

Mom

I looked up to find Sam flipping an omelet in a pan in a graceful maneuver using only the pan. I folded the letter and slipped it back into the worn envelope. My eyes brimmed with tears that I tried to hold back, and I took a deep breath to calm myself before speaking.

"Sam, thank you for keeping this," I said.

"Don't worry. I didn't read it," he replied as he gently dropped the omelet onto the plate. "No mushrooms—only peppers, some feta, and spinach. Your mom mentioned you didn't like mushrooms when I tested out my mushroom risotto recipes on them for a week."

"Thanks. I wondered how you knew our kitchen so well," I noted, trying to really *see* him, this man with the motorcycle and the dog, cooking me breakfast.

"Oh yeah, I used to cook here a lot—like risotto week. Henry and Annette were great about letting me test out new recipes on them. Do you want to talk about it? The letter, I mean."

I sniffed to keep the tears away, hoping Sam would get the point, and changed the subject. "You're the guy...with the painting...in your restaurant downtown," I said, putting the pieces together. Mom must have wanted to tell me but assumed that I'd never believe it. I wouldn't have, of course. That peculiar story would have pushed me straight into Adam's arms—anything to avoid conforming to my "great" destiny. She knew me, I thought.

"Oh, Annette told you about the painting? My old boss gave it to me when I left, said it reminded him of me. I guess he found it on a trip in New York. I don't know anything about art, but I like it."

"So, my mom didn't tell you?" I asked.

"Tell me what?" he replied.

"About the artist?" I asked, now starting to feel increasingly unsure by the second.

"No, she didn't mention anything. Why? Should I know who the artist is? Someone named Morningside."

I couldn't help myself. Some part of me needed him to know everything about me, probably the part of me that noticed how very enchanting his eyes were. Really I didn't need to stare because I knew those eyes almost better than my own, having spent hours painting them and testing out colors to get them exactly right. "Oh...um...I thought she would have said…It's…me, actually. *I'm* Morningside. It's how I sign my paintings anyway. I live…I used to live near Morningside Park in the city. I wanted a New York name for my work, I guess. Sounds silly, probably." I cringed.

"Wow, you painted that? It's really good! Who's the guy? He sure looks a *lot* like me…and rides the same color motor-cycle…and the dog is practically a spitting image of Neb. Everyone who sees it thinks that I commissioned someone to do it."

Because it *is* you, I thought. The dreams, Mom's letter, the darts…My scientific mind wrestled with my heart, and science was losing big time. Sam was charming, handsome, and…perfect. I knew I was in trouble. "Um…well…art is…subjective, and a lot of people see themselves in that painting actually. It's been very popular."

He looked like he didn't believe that explanation. "Right."

I didn't know what to say. "Mom wrote in the letter that she wants me to meet some chief in Seaside. We've never been connected to the tribe; at least I didn't think we were." I stopped.

"Seaside, huh? There's a good motorcycle shop there that I've been meaning to check out. Maybe we could go together," he said simply, standing in the kitchen as if we'd been living together for years. It was disorienting.

"Great omelet, by the way. Thanks for cooking. Why didn't you find a more modern house, closer to the restaurant? I mean, this neighborhood is great, but the houses are all his-toric relics, built in the 1890s."

"That was what I would call another sign, but you'd probably call it coincidence. My realtor found the restaurant first really easily—a real kismet opportunity. Then I hoped for a house nearby, but only one house was on the market for six months straight. It was my only choice, so eventually I figured, why not? Wouldn't you know it? The day after I closed on the house, *twenty* properties came onto the market, and five in the area I was looking at. Weird, right?"

"Yeah, *that's* pretty weird," I said, unsure of what to say or do next, feeling pummeled by the loud signs from the universe that dwarfed those in Times Square. I felt as if the universe was yelling at me, and I didn't like being yelled at. Regardless, it couldn't be ignored.

"Of course, not like miracle-cure-superpower weird like your dog bite disappearing, but still pretty strange. It's as if the universe wanted me here, not only in *this* town, but in *that* house. You know what I think?"

"What do you think?" I tried to look normal as my heart raced.

He leaned over the counter slowly, moving his face in very close to mine. I took a deep breath. "I think…that fate brought me here, not only to Cape Disappointment, but to this *very* street. Fate brought me here to meet my soul mate, the love of my life and girl of my dreams." His eyes didn't break their close gaze, and I blinked first, suddenly looking away while my stomach twisted into all kinds of knots.

"I…uh…" I stammered and literally flinched. He quickly stepped back. I felt so uncomfortable. What was going on here? My pulse quickened, and my brain struggled to keep up.

"Oh! *You* think I was talking about *you*! Typical. A pretty girl like you thinks the *handsome* neighbor must be talking about *her*. Relax. The way I see it, it's probably Dorothy," he said matter-of-factly. I smiled and knew he had to be kidding. "I realize there's a bit of a May-December romance thing, but at least she's an Orioles fan." He grinned.

"May-December? She's old enough to be your grand-mother!" I knew he had to be kidding, but still I suddenly felt a little jealous.

"Every couple has its challenges," he said lightly with a wink. "Admit it, you're jealous."

"Of you and eighty-year-old *Dorothy*?" I asked, unsuccessfully attempting to cover up my thoughts.

"It's OK to be jealous. I mean, I'm the catch of the neighborhood, actually of the whole county. I know by your flinch that you still don't believe in fate."

"Flinch? I didn't—"

"Yeah, you flinched. It could have been seen from space. Like it scared the Hell, Michigan, out of you for a second there," he said confidently.

"Look, all my life I was raised with this wild story about me being a legendary keelalle, like I didn't have a choice in my life. I think our lives are what we make of them and that anything can happen. Fate to me means no choices, so no...I don't...I didn't...want anything to do with fate." That said, for his intense eyes, I could make an exception. I needed to get a grip.

"Well...Maybe for now only one of us needs to believe in fate. I'm happy for it to be me. After all, most women don't realize that I'm the love of their life when they first meet me, so I guess I'm used to it," he said blithely.

I chuckled. "You're used to it, huh?"

He grinned. I thought I was in trouble, and then I realized that trouble was already well in my rearview mirror. Sam made me *want* to believe in fate and soul mates and...*magic*.

The Tribe ❧ February

A few days passed quietly, and it was nice see the winter
storms finally subside. Gran, of course, kept me busy
with our constant time traveling: this morning I was ten, and
by lunchtime I was my mother.

Much of my energy focused on trying *not* to think about
Sam. Yesterday I spilled some soup on the floor after being distracted by watching him take Neb out for a walk. I had walked
over to the table and then saw him and couldn't look away or
think of anything else. Soon enough I noticed the spill and ran
quickly to wipe it up. This afternoon I let popcorn burn in the
microwave while watching him take down the Christmas lights
on Dorothy's house. Basically, I was becoming as distracted as
Gran, and pretty soon I'd need to pay someone to take care of
both of us. I had to get it together, I mused as I threw the popcorn in the garbage.

Soon there was a knock on the door, and I went to answer
it. Sam stood tall in the doorway, and I caught my breath. "Hi,"
I said while somewhat nervously pulling my ponytail out and
letting my hair fall.

"So, are you up for going to Seaside on Saturday then?" he asked.

"Yes," I said without thinking. Then I backpedaled. "Oh, um…Saturday? I don't even know what day *today* is, actually… I have to take care of Gran, so I——"

"How about I invite myself in and tell you all about my cunning plan?" He brushed my shoulder as he walked past me down the hallway. "What happened here? Hannah set the curtains of fire again?" he asked, commenting on the smell of burned popcorn.

What a great excuse, I thought. "She means well. Coffee?" I asked, holding up the coffee pot as he sat down at the table.

"Don't mind if I do. Thanks. Are you sure you don't want me to check the heater? Seems like it's hot over here today," Sam commented.

"Oh, it's probably only Gran messing with the thermostat. Thanks, though." I felt guilty about making poor Gran my scapegoat for everything today.

"Did you call the guy your mom wanted you to meet?" he asked.

"Yes, I did. It turns out that he's John Lane *Junior*. My mom's friend died a few years ago, but John Junior is the new council chairman. I'm sure she knew all of that. Anyway, he said he's happy to meet with me."

"So this chief is our age then?" he asked.

"I suppose so as our parents were the same age. And I'm pretty sure he doesn't go by 'Chief.'"

"And you're going to drive down there? It's almost an hour away. What about Hannah?"

"Oh, I don't know when I'll get over there. I'd have to take Gran with me of course, and she's not easy to schedule around."

He blinked quickly and avoided my eyes. "So here's my cunning plan. This morning I took down Dorothy's Christmas lights, and she asked if there was anything she could help me with in return. I asked her if she'd look after Hannah for a day so we could go to Seaside and Astoria."

"*And* Astoria?"

"Well, there's that nice bistro under the bridge, and I thought that we could go to dinner, you know, like a date." He fidgeted, seeming nervous.

I took a breath. "*Like* a date, or it would be a date?" I asked, buying time.

"OK, OK, I'll go on a date with you—jeez, stop asking me already," he said, laughing. "Have dinner with me, Kay."

I felt the butterflies in my stomach perform an air show. "And you're sure that Dorothy's OK with looking after Gran *all* day?"

"Yes, I'm sure. It was her idea, actually. She volunteered after I told her that I was hoping you'd join me for dinner. What can I say? She fell for my charm."

I knew that she wasn't the only one. "OK, yes. As long as Gran is taken care of, and you don't mind going to Seaside for a tribe visit, and I have no idea what that will be like…"

He smiled and replied, "It's a date then. I'll pick you up Saturday at two o'clock. Maybe I'll finally get to see you wearing something you haven't slept in."

I laughed. It was true that almost every time he'd seen me, I'd been basically wearing a sweatshirt and velour pants, hair falling out of a braid all askew, topped off with a robe and maybe some boots. And yet none of that seemed to matter.

He insisted on driving his motorcycle to Seaside, which seemed strange—and a little scary. What would I wear? I decided to wear black leather jeans and a white silk blouse, part of my "New York" clothes that Martina mailed me after I arrived on the Cape. Dorothy came by that morning, and soon Sam and I were in the driveway. It was still cold but the sky was completely clear and the snow was melting, which meant clear roads.

"Have you ridden a motorcycle before?" he asked.

"No, never. I'm a little afraid, actually," I confessed.

"OK, here's your helmet, and you'll sit behind me. Don't worry. I'm a good driver, and you'll be safe."

He showed me where to sit and gave me some tips about where to put my feet and how to lean into a turn. Soon we were off. At first we went slowly around the block, as Sam wanted to make sure I was OK, and then we hit the road. I leaned into him and held on tightly, and I soon considered driving cars to be highly overrated. He smelled like the ocean and pine trees, and I closed my eyes.

I considered selling my car and felt almost sad to arrive in Seaside only forty minutes later. We pulled into the driveway of John's house, a beautiful shingled cottage on the beach—a place that looked more in keeping with Martha's Vineyard than

Seaside. Suddenly we were in time with the rest of the world. John walked outside to greet us. He looked like an airbrushed movie star, strikingly attractive. I felt nervous meeting someone from the tribe that I've never been a part of.

"I'm glad you're here," I whispered to Sam. He smiled.

John bounded over to us. "So you must be Kehlok? I'm John. And this is?" He pointed at Sam.

"I'm Sam, the neighbor," he responded and offered a handshake.

"Sorry, *neighbor,* I'm afraid you can't join the council meeting. You'll have to wait out here or in the game room. There's a pool table and video games. I didn't realize Kehlok was bringing any company. Meeting is for tribe members only."

Sam seemed completely OK with this news. "That's fine. Do you want me to come back for you in an hour then?" he asked me, taking a step away.

Sam took a step closer to the motorcycle, and I reached out for his hand.

"Wait! Don't go." He looked both astonished and relieved. I looked over at John, feeling nervous but projecting an image of authority. "He's part of *my* tribe," I said boldly. I had no idea what I was doing exactly, only aware of a strong, completely irrational feeling that Sam wouldn't be separated from me. For whatever reason, I needed him to stay.

John looked disappointed. "Hey, it's just not done. I appreciate you want to bring your neighbor, but I don't make the rules."

"I am your keelalle, and it's either both of us or nothing," I said, even more self-assured. What were these archaic rules anyway? Sam stepped nervously, indicating that it was OK with him to leave. Still, I wouldn't change my mind.

John smiled. "A coyote spirit…the change-maker. We haven't had a coyote around here in a very, very long time. Your mom said you were a handful."

I grew up completely outside the tribe and thought my mom had too. Evidently, she had a lot of secrets. Everything I knew about the tribe was based on stories from Gran and Mom, when we were alone on a walk without Dad or Grandpa anywhere nearby. They both still respected the tribe lines, even inside the family.

I replied, still holding onto Sam's hand, which seemed to only make me feel bolder and more self-assured, "OK then. I'm sorry it couldn't work out. If the stories are true and I am the strongest, most powerful keelalle in two hundred years, then I could use your help, and you could probably use mine. But I've lived without the tribe's help my entire life, so what's the difference to me? Come on. Let's go, Sam." We put our helmets on and got back on the motorcycle.

"Wait!" John yelled loudly. We took the helmets off. John stepped closer to us. "Hold on a second. I said it *wasn't* done, not that it *couldn't* be done. After all, nature breaks what doesn't bend. If the chief and the keelalle can't change the rules, then who can? Welcome to the tribe, Sam," he said and shook his hand.

Sam touched my arm and whispered in my ear. "Are you sure about this?"

"I'm not *sure* about *anything*."

Great Wave ❖

*J*ohn led us to the living room at the back of the house, where a wall of patio doors overlooked the beach and ocean. The winds outside were unsteady, and the beach was covered with snow, but otherwise the sun shone through blue patches of sky. Clouds drifted across the view. Three people waited for us, two women and a man, lounging comfortably on leather sofas but quickly standing up for introductions and handshakes. John looked out of place with the others, who were all well over sixty. Evidently there were five on the council; another man named Earl couldn't make it because he was on vacation in Arizona.

Sam leaned in and whispered in my ear, "Looks like John and the cast of *Cocoon*," he joked. I stifled a smile and elbowed Sam to behave. It did look exactly like that, though. Everyone was polite to Sam after John's introduction, yet still a little unsure.

"Lovely view," I said, looking through the large patio doors. "It's nice of you all to come here to meet me."

"Wow, this house is incredible! You're right on the ocean," Sam exclaimed, evidently impressed.

"Thanks. Keeps the rain off," John replied casually. "Let me introduce everyone. Betty is a retired literature professor at Reed College, James is a retired lawyer, and Mary runs a B&B near Cannon Beach. I'm a senior software engineer, and I work from home. What do you do, Sam?" John asked politely.

"I'm a chef, so I don't really know anything about computers, except searching around the net for new recipes."

John looked him over closely. "I don't know anything about cooking, although I did develop a recipe app, but I'm sure we'll be good friends. Where are my manners? You guys must be tired. Please, sit down. How about a beer or soda?"

"Do you have any coffee?" I asked.

"Yes, of course. Sam, what would you like?" John asked politely.

"Coffee would be great, thanks."

"Two coffees coming up," John said, walking toward the kitchen. Sam followed.

The oldest woman in the group, Mary, was the most welcoming, and she stepped toward me once John and Sam left. She asked about Gran and explained that they had been childhood friends. Her eyes darkened, and she hugged me after I told her of Gran's dementia.

"My poor girl," Mary said kindly. "You have been left all alone in this without your mother or Hannah to help you. I am so very glad that you are here, my daughter. John was right to invite your friend too, I think." She smiled warmly, and I felt more at ease. John and Sam returned, smacking one another on the back like old sports buddies. We all soon sat down, and John began the discussion.

"As you all know, we gather today to welcome our keelalle and lost sister, Kehlok…um…and her *neighbor*, Sam. My father learned from his father, as it has been passed through the generations, that Kehlok is the direct descendent Saghalie Plah Tamahnous, the first coyote spirit, and also of Tamahna, the last of the most powerful keelalles, before the tribe joined the modern world."

I raised my hand like a grade-school student in class. Everyone looked at me strangely.

"Kehlok, you have a question?" Mary asked. "You don't have to raise your hand; simply speak. The council is an open forum, and you are a council member as keelalle."

"Oh, sorry. I…uh…what did you mean by saying that Tamahna was the *last* of the most powerful keelalles? I thought *all* keelalles were the same," I said, clearly a little confused.

John answered patiently, "Yes, Tamahna was the last of the *most* powerful, like Saghalie. Hasn't anyone ever told you about this?"

Sam looked at me reassuringly. "She's new at this whole tribe thing," he said with a smile.

John smiled in spite of himself and continued, "OK, well then, we'll start at the beginning. The tribe history explains that long ago the Clatsop were once a threatened tribe, nearly overtaken by the neighboring Chinook. The Chinook often stole our women and horses, raiding our camps and pushing us away from the river. One day, during a great battle, the Clatsop chief's daughter was injured and fled to the great mountain for safety. She drank the mountain waters and found herbs to heal her wounds. On the mountain she was alone for a very long time until she befriended a coyote, her spirit animal."

"A *coyote*? My ancestor befriended a coyote?" I interrupted, clearly in disbelief and instantly aware of why Mom called me her coyote-girl.

Sam chuckled. "Like I said, she's new at this. Please continue…Chief…um…sir? What do we call you?" Sam asked.

John raised his eyebrows. "You can call me John," he replied with a smile. "Yes, the coyote listened to her stories of her tribe and decided to help her. He brought her sacred water to drink from the mountain snow and gave her three powers to protect her tribe. Coyote gave her the power to influence the weather, the power to heal others with nature, and the power to see the future. When she returned to her tribe from the great mountain, she knew when the Chinook were planning to attack, and she started a powerful and devastating lightning storm that hit their villages. Finally, she healed the tribe's warriors of their previous battle wounds, and the Clatsop grew very strong. Her name was Saghalie Plah Tamahnous, which means 'lightning magic.' Her four-times great-granddaughter was Tamahna, the last of the keelalle to have all three powers."

"She controlled the weather?" I asked incredulously. "No wonder mom didn't tell me this story. It's absurd."

"According to legend, she protected the people and the land from the great wave."

"The great wave?" Sam asked.

Mary looked over at James, another council member, for the answer. James explained, "The tsunami of 1700, caused by the eight-point-seven Cascadia earthquake—that tsunami would have devastated the area if Saghalie hadn't used her powers to hold the great, raging seas back from the shore. That earthquake was as powerful as the one in the Indian Ocean that caused the tsunami in Indonesia in 2004; basically, it would have been catastrophic for all tribes living on the coast. Old fishermen like me know a lot about meteorology. They say those earthquakes of magnitude eight or nine have hit our coast every three to five hundred years. The last Cascadia quake was well over three hundred years ago, so we're due," James explained.

"So, you're saying that Saghalie held the tsunami back? A tsunami like the one in Indonesia?" I asked. "And she talked to coyotes? I mean, that sounds a little—"

John nodded. "We're only telling you the tribe legends, our history—*your* history."

"You must understand that Saghalie was *very* powerful," James said. "Legend says that she pushed the waters back until only a calm sea moved into the coast, breaking the wave in half before it made landfall. With our traditions, we have only the oral tradition of stories, many of which were turned into songs."

"Because songs are easier to remember," Sam said. "I'll never forget the song that was playing during my first kiss." He quickly stopped himself. I was grateful for the interruption, though.

"Yes, songs are certainly easier to remember," James responded. "Do you want to hear Saghalie's song?"

"I would. Kay? What about you?" Sam asked.

"Um…Sure."

"I defer to Betty; she's the best singer among us. Betty? Would you mind?" James asked.

"OK, here goes. Now let me see if I can do it justice." Betty stood up, and everyone looked at her, waiting expectantly.

Mary smiled and clapped and then said, "I love this song. *All* Clatsop learn this as children, like the other stories passed down from generation to generation. You probably already know it, Kehlok. I'm sure your mother sang it to you."

Everyone nodded in agreement while Betty remained perceptibly composed. She began:

> She heard the roar 'fore the quake
> Coyote taught her to listen and to see
> In a vision she saw the great wave
> She felt the power of the sea
>
> The wind howled yet she stood tall
> Saghalie held fast like a mountain
> Soon the great wave calmed so small
> We remained our many thousand
>
> She heard the roar 'fore the quake
> Saghalie turned the power of the sea
> So strong she would not break
> Saghalie turned the power of the sea
>
> Cascadia bowed and turned
> diving deep back into the sea
> Cascadia bowed and turned
> diving deep back into the sea

We clapped in appreciation. Betty's presentation was outstanding. I could imagine her students sitting in rapt attention while she read from *Hamlet* or *The Great Gatsby*.

"I remember that now. Mom used to sing that to me when I was little. Lou always messed up the words: 'She stirred green eggs for the cake' instead of 'She heard the roar 'fore the quake,'" I commented with a laugh. "He annoyed mom so much that she eventually stopped singing it."

Mary nodded. "Yes, the *boy* was never destined to learn the old ways," she noted, clearly sharing Gran's bias.

"Hey, that's my brother," I said in his defense.

Mary continued, ignoring my protest, "If only Hannah had prevailed and convinced Annette not to let you move to New York, things would be so different now. There would have been more time. Annette must have seen it. She was irresponsible. She should never have let you grow up outside the tribe."

Thunder roared across the beach outside, and a flash of lightning lit up the sky. I stared harshly at Mary. She had no right to say such things, and anger stirred throughout my being. "Don't you dare talk about my mother," I said. Thunder clapped again, edging closer.

Mary smiled fiendishly and looked at the patio doors to the storm; then she looked knowingly at John. "I'm sorry, Kehlok. I didn't mean it. I just wanted to try something. Did you notice that thunder, on such a clear day?"

John nodded in response, looking like he'd seen a ghost.

"You're seriously talking about the weather right now? What's wrong with you?" This woman was crazier than Gran.

"I can't believe you'd say that about my mother. It was a mistake for me to come here." I put my jacket on.

"Wait!" John stood up quickly and walked over to me, kneeling down by my chair. "Kehlok, this is going to sound a little strange, and I wouldn't have believed it if I hadn't just... well...seen *that*. Mary was testing you."

"Testing me? By being rude and insulting?" I asked. "What is this? Some sort of sophomoric initiation ceremony?"

"Mary was testing to see if the legend could be true—if you have the third power. Theoretically, you should be able to influence the natural elements, like Saghalie and Tamahna. It was foretold that the fifth-generation keelalle after Tamahna would regain all three powers, and she would be the first coyote spirit the tribe had seen in ten generations since the first, Saghalie Plah Tamahnous. Legends say that her power to influence the weather was tied to her emotions. Once she was mad at her brother, and lightning hit his house," John explained.

"I'm not saying that I believe any of this, but how was this power that you think Kay has somehow lost in the previous generations?" Sam asked.

I stood up and walked over toward the hallway; Sam quickly followed. "Now you're saying that I can *control* the weather? What's next? The tooth fairy is my cousin? Talking bears? What? It was a mistake to come here."

Sam placed his hand on the small of my back, and I started to calm down. As he leaned in closer to me, I felt like a ship pulled into a safe harbor. He guided me back to a sofa and sat down beside me, and I almost forgot about being upset.

James smiled at Sam. "Thank you, Sam. I see the weather has cleared up quickly, now that the storm has passed." Both John and Mary nodded in quick agreement. I felt like everyone else understood something that still was beyond my reach.

Outside, the gray sky had faded into blue with only a few light clouds. Mary spoke. "There is much you do not know, child. Don't judge what you don't yet understand. The coyote spirit is the change-maker, the creator of worlds. Before humans lived on the earth, our legends say that animal people were here. The coyote was the first of the animals to talk, and he taught the others. Coyote and Raven created our world, and they occasionally intervened to help our people."

Betty added, "Kay, there are many creation stories throughout the world, as you know. Clatsop legends have some that say that Coyote created the Columbia River, and Raven created the other streams. These are the stories of time and our people, not much different from other cultures and religions. For example, the Christians have God, who created the world in seven days; the Hindus have Brahma; the ancient Egyptians had Ra; and the ancient Greeks had Gaia. All of these myths and legends grew from local understanding and were passed down for generations in stories, much like ours. There's something human about explaining our world creatively, and at the end of the day, there is no single explanation. Most of us believe a composite."

James nodded in agreement, saying, "The coyote and raven stories are simply part of our history and how the tribe understood the world. Tamahna was a raven spirit, a magical changer like Coyote. A raven spirit itself is magical—and very rare, like

Coyote. Tamahna's twin soul was destined to be Meriwether Lewis, a white man who changed everything."

"Hold on, you mean Meriwether Lewis as in the 'Lewis' of Lewis and Clark?" Sam interrupted.

"Kehlok didn't tell you? Yes, Tamahna's twin soul was Meriwether Lewis. Their daughter could heal others, but she could not see the future nor control the weather. Tamahna was devastated when Lewis was killed, and her constant tears changed the weather permanently. He had promised to return to her after completing his time as governor, although he initially hoped to return right after the expedition. Jefferson had other plans."

"Sorry to keep interrupting, but I though Lewis committed suicide," Sam stated.

"None of us believe that, including the Lewis family," I said. "They've been working to clear his name with a forensics examination for many years now. Unfortunately, it's stuck in a legal battle."

James continued. "Anyway, before Lewis, weather here was beautiful with enough rain, but not *daily* rain. Tamahna's grief cursed the area, and it has rained almost daily since Lewis left. Even in the journals by the members of the Discovery Corps, you can see that. Patrick Gass from the expedition wrote a weather report every day, and during the entire time they were at Fort Clatsop, there were maybe two days of rain. That grief of lost love impacted Tamahna's daughter and future generations, when eventually the powers were lost in a generation. Legend said that it would take both another coyote spirit and a raven spirit to be born before all the powers would return to the tribe."

Mary added, "And legends also say that a keelalle can communicate telepathically with the chief, allowing them to warn the tribe of danger. We think that power is lost too but that it will return again. You must now understand which power Hannah has and your mother has, right?"

"Gran was always a natural healer, and my mom learned things through her, but she always struggled with natural remedies. Mom always knew what was going to happen next though; it was uncanny."

"Yes, your mother could see into the future, and Hannah could heal others. You, my dear, a true coyote spirit, will exceed both of their abilities," Mary explained.

"But you said the legend required both a coyote spirit and a raven spirit. Who's the raven?" I asked.

"I am," John replied. "First raven spirit in the tribe in two hundred years."

James added, "John is known as Tyee Kaka Kloshe Nanitch. Do you know what that means, Kehlok?"

"Of course—Chief Raven Guard. I might not have grown up with the tribe, but my mom and Gran made sure that I learned the old language," I replied a little too defensively.

"Yes, it is a pity that you did not grow up within the tribe, but there were...reasons why it had to be. Anyway, that's why he is chief today, despite his *very* young age. Chief is not a hereditary title, like keelalle is; a chief is elected. We selected John to replace his father, not because of heredity but because he is the first raven in two hundred years. His father *never* would have let Sam in today, for example. So already he's a change-maker." Sam shifted in his seat a bit while James looked at him somewhat disapprovingly.

"Now you understand how important you are," Mary said, trying to shift the conversation in a more positive direction. John coughed. "How important you *both* are."

"Thanks, Mary," John said with a smile. "Nice to be remembered." He laughed and everyone joined in.

"And I'll be able to control the weather. That doesn't sound crazy. No, not at all," I said sarcastically.

John corrected me, "Not *control*. More like *influence*."

"Oh, like that somehow sounds *less* nuts," I replied. "I don't understand why neither Mom nor Gran told me these stories."

"I think I understand, Kehlok," Mary volunteered. "Coyote spirits cannot be pushed; change-maker spirits must be *looking* for answers before they will accept them. Otherwise, they are not ready and rebel. Change-makers transform the world to themselves; other spirits adjust to the changes. They are the most independent of the spirits—fiercely independent."

I nodded. "Yes, that sounds *exactly* like me," I confirmed.

"Coyote and raven spirits are stubborn," James commented. "They are like the great sequoia trees: where a sequoia chooses to stand makes everything else around it adapt. A forest grows around it and the world is changed for centuries. Coyotes, especially, do not know how to follow. Your mother knew that telling you too much about your destiny would turn you against it. Because you came here looking for answers means that you should be able to accept them."

John smiled at me, recognizing a kindred spirit.

Coyote Spirit ❖

nd here I thought I'd grown up with all the information about the tribal history, yet I discovered how little I really knew. How did everyone *know* which animal spirit
belonged to any person? Why hadn't anyone told me about the
tsunami, twin souls, or the coyote creation myths? What kind
of medicine woman knows nothing about her tribe outside of
the old language and medicinal potions?

"How did *you* know that I am a coyote spirit?" I asked the
council members.

"Your mother saw it when you were very young. Don't you
remember?" John asked.

"I think I'd remember *coyotes*," I said dismissively. "I
thought it was just a nickname; they often called me 'coyote
girl' because of all the trouble I got into."

John continued. "Your mother and my father were very
close and were going to be married until your mother met her
twin soul. Their breakup was very difficult for my dad, even
after he met my mother and married. That's another reason
why you were not raised with the tribe; your mother thought it
would be too painful for my dad as chief."

"I sometimes wondered about that. All the legends that I grew up with but no tribe…Mom had more secrets than I realized. So by 'twin soul,' you mean soul mate?" I asked.

"Yes. A keelalle's twin soul, or soul mate, is drawn to her like a magnet. It's sad for anyone in their path between, like my father, because what seems like love is only a shadow. A keelalle's power comes from the love of Coyote, the creator of worlds and source of all things. Love is what pulls a keelalle's twin soul to her from across tribes or, in Tamahna's case, across the known world, with Meriwether Lewis." John looked at Sam and then back at me, clearly suspecting, like myself, that Sam was more than my neighbor. "Twin souls make the keelalles *more* powerful. Most keelalles are limited until their twin souls arrive in their lives—kind of like a superpower booster," John said playfully.

The whole discussion started making me feel uncomfortable, as I saw everyone in the room eyeing Sam. "What about the coyotes?" I asked as a distraction.

"Like I said, Annette and my dad were once very close, and they managed to stay in touch, like once a year or so. We always got your family Christmas cards, so I feel like I know both you and your brother, Louis. Anyway, when you were two years old, she found you in the backyard, playing with a coyote that somehow had jumped the fence. Your mom had been in the kitchen, making some bread, when she looked up to see you laughing and toddling after the coyote like it was a Labrador retriever. She froze in terror, seeing you alone with it, petting it like a dog. She grabbed some pans and clanged them loudly from the patio door to scare the animal away. When it ran out of the yard, you started crying inconsolably for several hours, like a piece of you had been cut. That's when she called my dad for advice, and he told her not to worry, that the coyote would not hurt you. She should let you play with it, which she did when it returned. That's when the tribe realized that the magic would return; that you would be the keealle foretold by legends. Do you remember any of that?" John asked.

"I remember playing with a *dog* in the backyard and seeing dogs on our walks in the forest, but I don't remember any *coyotes*," I said.

"That's why then. You remember them as pets. Those weren't dogs; they were *coyotes*," Mary said emphatically. "Hannah used to comment all the time how frightened they would be with you out in the woods, petting coyotes around every corner. They did their best not to look afraid for your sake, and Hannah said she called them 'doggies' to make herself less afraid. Coyote spirits are a real challenge as children too—very independent, rebellious, willful, and playful. Your mother certainly had her hands full with you. She always said that your favorite phrase at even two years old was, 'I'll do it *myself.*'"

"I need to get some air," I said. I walked out the patio door to the beach. About twenty feet from the house, I found an enclosed patio on the beach and sat down in a chair to watch the waves roll in. Snow covered the edges of the patio and the roof, but the chairs were dry. Soon enough, John appeared and sat down next to me.

"Sam wanted to come out, but I pulled rank," he said and laughed. "It's a lot to digest, isn't it? I felt the same way when I found out that my dad had cancer and that they had appointed me chief. It was so strange, and I grew up with these people. I can't imagine how it is for you. Sorry. I shouldn't have invited the rest of the council, at least not for a first meeting. I thought it might be easier if you met everyone, but you kind of looked like a wild animal in a zoo cage, pacing and looking for a way out."

"If you bring up coyotes, I'm going home," I said sharply.

"Fair enough...So, Sam—he's your twin soul?"

"My mom thought so, and I guess I...um...I'm not sure what I think about him or any of this. There's a kind of magic around him—around *us*, I guess."

"As I suspected in the driveway, that means I *have* to accept him. A keelalle's twin soul must be *unconditionally* accepted by the chief, or the tribe suffers. Sometimes their twin souls appeared from rival tribes or even, once, a traveling sailor; and of course there was the last paleface, Meriwether Lewis," John explained. "Don't worry. I'll make Sam my new best friend, and the rest of the tribe will follow. They know the rules."

"This is too much. I came back from New York after losing Mom and Dad, and there are all these strange things that I don't understand—things that I thought I knew, you know, like me and my family. I spent my entire life running away from this...this *prophecy*. I cured a dog bite in a day, like magic; it disappeared completely, as if nothing happened. And now I'm talking about meeting my soul mate and influencing the weather with special powers like some hippie on a trip."

"It *does* sound bonkers, but that's what you're supposed to be able to do, according to legend anyway. Look, I'm a software engineer, and I live in the real world, like you. My girlfriend, Aiko, is a Japanese Buddhist, and we eat sushi, go salsa dancing, and occasionally text each other from different rooms in the same house. Through it all, I'm still also the raven chief trying to figure out what to do with the new medicine woman and working with our congresswoman to get the tribe formally recognized again. On the one hand, it all sounds a bit mental, but on the other, it's life, which is both messy and miraculous. It's OK that we're not sure about any of this. If you were completely sure, I'd probably be compelled to check you into a mental hospital."

I laughed. "Gee, thanks."

"I only wanted to let you know that I know how hard this is. You're dealing with the loss of your parents and what that means for you as a person, which is heavy. And then we tell you that you can probably change the weather…which would be a lot for anyone to manage. All I can tell you is the advice my mom gave me, which is to start small. Don't try to figure *everything* out in one day. Start small. The rest will work itself out."

"Thanks, Tyee Kaka Kloshe Nanitch. You know, you're pretty wise for someone so young. What are you, like sixteen?"

"Ha-ha, very funny. And call me John; I don't like titles. When I was growing up, my dad used to call me *Hoolhool*, because I was like a mouse, always only eating cheese." He laughed. "I guess that's really the native name I feel most comfortable with, but the tribe said that they didn't want a Tyee

Hoolhool. Wouldn't be respectable. And…I'm only a *few* years younger than you."

"You remind me of my little brother, actually, Hoolhool." I laughed at the name. "Hey, don't tell the others on the council, but I have been working on something."

"Really?"

"I've been trying to heal Gran's Alzheimer's, which I know sounds absurd, but I try anyway. Every day I test out different concoctions on her, and sometimes there's an improvement, but then another deeper slide into it a day later. Nothing really seems to work. If I am this super keelalle, then why can't I help her?"

"Keelalles can't save everyone," John explained. "Even the most powerful, like Saghalie Plah Tamahnous, who lost her mother to a terrible illness—the night of the tsunami, actually. The most powerful can't save everyone; it's not meant to be."

"Why didn't any of this start when I was younger? I mean, why now? Science and medicine were always easy for me, even when I was a kid. I pushed to do art because it challenged me. Still, as a kid I'd never done anything like heal a dog bite overnight or somehow make thunder roar."

"Mary's theory is that you wanted to save your parents more than you wanted to live, and that's the type of love that flips a switch and starts the transition. She said that your gran wanted to save her husband, who was injured at sea. And your mom wanted to save her brother, who died climbing Mount Rainier."

"I remember. Uncle Steve—he was so much fun. Mom was different after he died. She blamed herself."

"Combine your parents' deaths with meeting Sam, and you've got some serious energy, or whatever, working on you. It's chilly out here; do you think that you could change that?"

"I wouldn't even know how to try. If I am actually influencing the weather, then I have no idea how I'm doing it."

"How'd you do it earlier?"

"I didn't *do* anything. I was angry at Mary for what she said about Mom, but it's not like I wiggled my nose or anything."

John looked at me with disbelief. "Sure, that thunderstorm that lasted *two* minutes just happened without you doing anything. And this snow for *weeks* on the Oregon coast? When has that *ever* happened? Typically we get maybe three inches of snow in an entire year; since your parents passed away, the area has been hit by almost two feet of snow—I don't think that's a coincidence."

"Honestly, I didn't…I don't know what you want from me."

"You really don't know how you did it, do you? So, you were angry before; let's experiment. It's only you and me out here; Raven and Coyote *kickin'* it on the beach. Close your eyes and think about Sam. Come on. Try."

I sighed. It sounded outrageous. I closed my eyes and thought of Sam. "Anything happening?"

"Tell me about him. What do you like about him?"

I couldn't help but smile, still keeping my eyes closed. "Sam is funny, confident, and ruggedly handsome. He smells like the ocean and pine trees, and he remembers little things, like that I don't eat mushrooms. He's like a safe harbor of warm and quiet water."

"OK, open your eyes."

"For the record, this was a *ridiculous* idea."

"No, it wasn't. Look up. The snow has melted off the patio roof completely and on the top part of the beach near the house. Not a cloud in the sky."

I gasped. "That's impossible."

"In love, *all* things are possible. Also, legends say that the raven spirit is magical. So who knows? Maybe it's our combined superpowers at work here. At least we can confirm that your emotions are somehow the base of how you influence the weather. I wouldn't have believed it myself if I didn't see it. Anger means thunder, sadness is snow, and happiness brings the sunshine. We're totally inviting you to *all* the tribe picnics now!" He chuckled.

"Ha-ha. But what am I supposed to do with all of this? Why me? What if this isn't merely a bunch of mysterious coincidences? Then what? Do I have to move to Seaside and run tribe meetings? What? I have this…ability…so I can improve the weather?"

"Steady now. Nothing like this has happened in *ten* generations. No one knows what it all means or what you're supposed to do. We'll figure it out. You'll find your way, and at least you're not alone. You have a group of at least six people on this planet who believe in this crazy story."

"Six? But there are only five on the council."

"Adding in the paleface. He seems totally on board with this. You know, I think you could tell him that your cousin is the tooth fairy, and he'd roll with it."

I laughed for a quick second and then stopped short. "Yeah, he has been cool with all of this, but I worry that it's some sort of spell. It seems too…too…perfect with Sam, so I don't know how to trust it. But then, at the same time, I completely trust it."

"Yep, you're a mess," John said, grinning. "That's the way I feel about Aiko. She's way too cool about me being chief, and I keep waiting for her to say it's all too much and walk away."

I sighed. "Sam believes in fate, and he's fine with all of this. It's an adventure for him, I guess."

"But for you, it's a box," John replied.

"Exactly. For me it means more than soul mate, it means talking coyotes and believing in…everything."

"When my dad found out that I was a raven spirit, Mom had to stop him from writing to the president; he was so excited. I freaked out and went to MIT to study engineering and real, practical things that made sense."

"I ran away from home too," I said. "I guess James was right about change-maker spirits; we are stubborn and create our own path."

"Right. Like a sequoia, we took our time, yet we both made a decision to return to our roots in Clatsop lands. We'll figure this out…*together*, Raven and Coyote." John smiled and I did too. "Who knows? Maybe we'll be the first in generations to reestablish the keelalle-chief telepathic hotline."

"I don't know if I've made that decision yet...to stay in Clatsop lands anyway. But you know something? I'm glad that I came here today. I felt really nervous about it and like a stranger, but now I see that I'm not alone in this."

"No, you're not. Come on. Let's go inside. They must be beside themselves, wanting to know what's going on."

"Can we keep this to ourselves, for now at least, this whole snow-melting thing? I don't want to explain it to Sam—or any-one—just yet."

John looked over at the patio doors. "Too late! The cat's already out of the bag. We have an audience."

I looked over to see the rest of the council and Sam stand-ing by the patio doors, pointing at us. "Right, well, at least for now let's not tell them *what* we were talking about."

"That's fine with me." We joined the others back inside.

The room buzzed with energy with everyone asking about the snow. Sam looked at me and instantly seemed to sense how tired I was, almost before I even realized it. I felt like I had been up all night studying for exams; I was so tired that I had to sit down. I remembered having felt the same way after talking to Kristin and after healing the dog bite. Great, one more thing I couldn't explain and didn't understand, the list of which grew by the minute. I had to sit down.

"All right, everyone, I think it's time for me to take Dances-with-Coyotes back to Astoria. We have a dinner date, and I'll be unable to sweep her off her feet if my valentine is exhausted, so we better head out."

I looked at Sam, in complete agreement about leaving, but I had one last question for the council. "Do you know where Meriwether Lewis's journals are?" I asked.

"Hannah and your mom didn't tell you where they were?" Mary asked, concerned.

"No, they didn't. Mom's gone now, and Gran is…Well, she's physically there, but most of the time, she's gone. I've been asking her about them whenever she's lucid, but I don't think she can remember. Any time I ask her about it, she tells me to ask my mom," I explained.

Everyone looked at each other, clearly alarmed.

John added, "Dad didn't even know. I asked him about it before he passed away. He said that only keelalles knew the location and that the journals were moved every generation, to keep them safe."

"They are certainly *safe*, considering that no one knows where they are," Sam joked, playfully tapping my shoulder.

"That's for sure. I'll keep trying to find out where they are, but if any of you remember anything, a clue, please let me know."

"I don't think we can help at all. Hey, isn't your brother a whale spirit?" James responded seriously.

"Yeah, he is. How do you guys know about all the animal spirit stuff, anyway? Is there like some sort of secret native handshake thing you need to teach me?"

James laughed. "Nothing like that. Mainly the parents tell the council leaders, so we all just know. It's the parents who figure it out, watching how you interact with nature when you're a child."

"Why would Lou be able to help me find the journals if he's been out of the loop with all of this tribe stuff like me?" I felt even more confused.

"A whale spirit is the keeper of knowledge and records. The whale spirit holds the memories of the ocean and her creatures for all eternity," James explained.

"Oh…I thought it meant that he liked being in the water," I said.

Everyone laughed. "Kehlok, you still have a lot to learn, don't you?" John said.

"I guess so."

John continued. "As James said, a whale spirit is the record keeper, and we need to find the journals, so maybe he can tap into something to help you find them. Your mother would have left clues that only *you* could decipher, Kehlok, to make sure the journals would not be lost forever."

"When Lou gets home, we'll see what we can figure out. If I do find them, does the council approve that they should be published as they are, no edits?" I asked because I felt I should.

Everyone looked to John, as clearly his authority on this issue was known and uncontested. "We've discussed this issue when we found out that your mother had passed away and realized they could be lost. Yes, they should be published; the world is ready for the truth and technology has finally advanced enough to prove their authenticity."

"I'm glad we agree," I said. "OK, well, we should go. Thanks for everything. It was really wonderful to meet you all. I feel like I have a whole other family."

"The tribe is family, and we're here for you, Kehlok," John said as he walked us out to the driveway.

Hospital Visit ❋

fter the council meeting, we returned north to Astoria. The weather was cold but wonderfully crisp, without rain. In Astoria, we first stopped to visit Kristin in the hospital. At the hospital door, I stopped for a few seconds before entering. This visit was my first time back to the hospital since November, when I'd rushed here to find my parents, when I'd met Sam and essentially taken custody of Gran. This building was the end of so many things and the beginning of others. I watched the automatic doors open and close in front of us, as I stopped for a minute.

"Are you OK?" Sam asked patiently.

"It's just this building, you know? I haven't been here since…November."

"Try to not see death here, Kay; see life and miracles. Change your focus. This is where a miracle happened in my life, and I met you. This building is where your friend is healing after a lifesaving surgery, thanks to you. You can do this," he encouraged. "Come on; we'll go in together," he said, reaching for my hand. I took it and nodded. We moved forward through the doors together.

Our first stop was the gift shop to get some flowers. Once in Kristin's room, we found her sleeping. I noticed the windows provided a nice view of the landmark Astoria-Megler Bridge, which we'd crossed earlier that day. Kristin's husband, Leon, sat in a chair near her bed, reading a mystery novel. He stood up when we arrived and smiled upon seeing me.

"Kay, it's great to see you. She's been asking for you. The surgery went incredibly well, and they are optimistic that they removed all the cancerous tissue. If you hadn't told her to get tested, we never would have found this so early and at such an operable stage. It's a *miracle*, and I want to thank you. I can't even imagine. If we had waited even a few months to find it had spread..." His voice trailed off.

"I'm glad she's OK," I said, reaching out to hold her hand. "Leon, you remember Sam, right?"

"Of course, from the——" He avoided finishing with *funeral* for my benefit.

"Yes. I'm glad to hear that Kristin's well," responded Sam quickly.

"She looks good," I commented, watching Kristin sleep peacefully. I took off my jacket and set it on the chair.

"Yes, she does. You must have the same touch as your mother. Annette often brought me cases from the clinic for referrals. And I also called her up from the clinic every now and then for consults on unusual cases. Although she wasn't a doctor, she saved a lot of lives with her natural ability to diagnose the most puzzling cases. It was like she could see the future."

"Mom could always see things...that other people missed." I corrected myself before saying something strange about her keelalle ways.

"I don't know how she did it, but eventually we stopped asking. Kristin thinks you have the same ability, and, after your latest help with her, I agree."

"I don't know about that," I said modestly. "It was more likely a lucky guess."

"Was it, Kay?" Sam asked. "Leon, what are the odds that someone would have identified Kristin's case that early?"

Leon answered quickly. "Impossible-to-one odds. As a doctor, I don't use the word *miracle* very often, but that's what it was. In fact, there is a patient in pediatrics that I'd like you to consult on, Kay."

Sam tugged on my sleeve, confidently. I stammered, "I'm not...it's only that...I haven't—"

Leon continued disregarding my hesitation. "He's been diagnosed with possible multiple sclerosis, but none of us feel confident in that diagnosis. It's the best we have, and we'll continue more tests, but all I could think last week was that I wished I could call Annette. Would *you* mind seeing him?"

"We came here to see Kristin," I said, politely indicating that, yes, I would mind.

"I know. But she's resting now, and it's best not to wake her. Why don't we take a walk over to pediatrics, and you can see the patient. By the time we get back, Kristin might be awake," Leon suggested.

Sam walked over to the window. "I don't know, Leon. Kay might not be ready for that. This is her first visit to the hospital since November, when her——" He stopped short. He turned around to look at me; Sam wouldn't push me. He waited.

"Of course, Kay, please don't feel obligated. If anyone needs some magic today, though, it's that kid. I suppose that I'm just grasping at straws."

I thought about it; a part of me knew *instinctively* that I could help. *And I should help.* "OK, sure. I'll be happy to consult, although you know that I'm not a licensed osteopathic physician. I've completed med school, but not the exams for a DO certification."

Sam beamed and walked back toward me. "That's my girl," he whispered proudly. "Come on, Dances-with-Coyotes. Let's kick the tires and see what you can do."

"Kay, it's just a consult like in med school. I'll be there with you," Leon explained.

"OK," I nodded and then shivered. Sam put his hand on my face to push some stray hairs away from my eyes.

"Terrific—let's go then. You know, we could really use another osteopath here at the hospital if you're looking for a job, presuming you get your license, of course."

Down the hallway we heard a loud beeping noise combined with the rush of footsteps and carts being moved into a nearby room. My blood started to turn to ice, and I stopped in my tracks. Sam turned back for me and reached for my hand. "You're *freezing*. Here, take my jacket." I put his jacket on but still felt the cold of death emanating from that room. I knew they could not save the patient, who was already gone. Sam put his arm around and rubbed my arms to warm me. Taking a deep breath, I took his arm and walked beside him, feeling stronger.

We continued along the occasional land mines of death's doors until we reached the young patient Leon wanted me to meet. Inside the room, we saw a young boy who looked to be four or five years old with dishwater-blond hair, sitting up in the bed while playing on a tablet. Leon introduced us to the boy's mother first.

"Mrs. Bailey, I've brought in a friend of mine who's a specialist in alternative-medicine therapies. Would you mind if she spoke with Tyler for a few minutes?"

Mrs. Bailey looked at Sam and me, and she seemed willing to try anything for her son. She nodded.

"Hey, Tyler," Leon said.

"Hi, Dr. Leon. Who are they?" Tyler asked, looking up briefly from his tablet.

"These are my friends, Kay and Sam. Do you mind if they talk to you for a few minutes?"

"OK," Tyler said, pausing his game on the tablet and setting it down.

Sam pushed me to the bedside, and I tried to smile. Tyler reminded me a little of Kristin's son, Grady, so I tried to pretend that I was talking to Grady. I remembered my university days and our clinic sessions meeting patients.

"What's your game?" I asked.

"It's called Caterpillar Pillars, and it's about building things. I'm going to be a builder like my dad when I grow up," he said.

"Wow! You *already* know what you want to be when you grow up," I exclaimed. "I'm still trying to figure that out myself."

"Mom says I'm an old soul," Tyler said and shrugged casually.

I smiled, trying not to laugh. "Do you have other games on there too?" I asked, indicating the tablet.

"Yeah, it's got everything on here. See?" He held up the tablet to show me, opening up a crossword puzzle. My thoughts flashed to the puzzle boxes, and I saw "ABCD" listed, but after I blinked, the boxes were empty. *ABCD…ABCD.* My thoughts raced to untangle what that meant while Tyler continued to demonstrate the tablet's capabilities like a trained salesman. *A gene—it was a gene!* I couldn't quite remember what it meant exactly.

"Thanks, Tyler. You'll be my go-to guy when I decide to buy a tablet," I said. "Thanks for letting me talk to you today."

"No problem. At least you're not like the other doctors who look so serious and want to poke me with needles all the time. I like *you*," Tyler said.

"I like you too. Take care," I said as I walked toward the door. Leon thanked Mrs. Bailey, and we walked around the corner, stopping outside the nurses' station.

"Well?" asked Leon expectantly.

"This is going to sound odd…I don't know. It's probably nothing, Leon."

"Let *me* determine that. *What* is probably nothing?" he asked.

"His ABCD-one gene…related to oil?" I shook my head, trying to remember. "Something about the gene, and there's an oil treatment. What is it? I can't remember."

"ABCD-*one*," Leon confirmed.

"Yes…I wish I could remember the connection; it's rare and often presents as multiple sclerosis."

I could see Leon's mind racing as he muttered something about proteins and fatty acids. "Kay, that's incredible. It's Lorenzo's oil! If you're right, then we have a chance to cure him. It's still so early that it's almost undetectable." Leon leaned in to the nurse behind the desk. "Pamela, get me a plasma VLCFA test for Tyler as soon as possible. I want to see if there are any elevations."

"Yes, Doctor," the nurse said.

"And I'm writing this down for Dr. Williamson. Make sure he sees this on rounds today. It's possible that Tyler has adrenoleukodystrophy, or ALD, *not* MS. Talk to Mrs. Bailey about getting the immediate family screened for HLA. If it's ALD, Tyler will need a bone-marrow transplant as soon as possible. Once you get the VLCFA results, send a copy of Tyler's records over to the Krieger Institute in Baltimore for a second opinion."

"I'll take care of it, and we'll have Dr. Williamson page you when he rounds," the nurse replied efficiently.

"Thanks," Leon said. "I'm going back to my wife's room; it's in the roster, but I have my pager with me, of course." Pamela acknowledged with a single head nod and typed notes in the computer.

"Let's head back and see if Kristin is awake." Leon started walking quickly, and Sam put his arm around me again to usher me through the hall. "I'm so impressed, Kay, and you do have your mother's touch. If you're right, and we've caught it in time, a bone-marrow transplant could help that kid live a normal life. ABCD-one is the gene that causes ALD."

"ALD from Lorenzo's oil...Yes, *that's* what I was trying to remember!"

"Kristin was right. You are a prodigy," Leon said excitedly.

"I don't think that...It was a lucky guess, and besides, we don't know if it's right yet."

"ALD!" Leon exclaimed. "Yes, that makes sense. I think you're right, and *luck* has nothing to do with it."

Back in Kristin's room, we found her still asleep. I didn't want to wake her, so I left a note and told Leon that I'd try to come back again soon. He knew how difficult it was for me to get out of the house without Gran, and he thanked us for coming.

"Sam, hope to see you around again soon for that basketball game we talked about."

Under the Bridge ❦

I nearly skipped out of the hospital, happy to leave it behind me, yet still a little annoyed with Leon for volunteering me to work on mysterious medical cases. The responsibility scared me.

We drove downtown, stopping at the docks adjacent to the bistro under the Astoria-Megler Bridge, with its industrial-green steel trusses spanning the Columbia River. The recent rainstorms had cleared most of the snow off the sidewalks and streets, leaving behind only spotted piles. For February, the day was unseasonably warm and sunny. The weather had been crazy in the area since I'd moved back. We'd had snow, hail, and then today clear sunshine. What if I *was* influencing things?

"I like that my coat smells like you now," he said after I returned it to him as we stopped to gaze at the periwinkle- and lavender-shaded sunset over the gray-blue water.

I couldn't help but smile, and he leaned in closer to kiss me. When his lips touched mine, I was pretty sure the earth stopped turning; in the entire universe of particles, beings, sound, and light, we were alone, floating. Maybe it was a minute, an hour, or a day; all I knew at the end of that kiss was that it would forever mark time. There were the black-and-white days before the kiss and the high-definition Technicolor days after it, and nothing would ever be the same.

He only shook his head, catching his breath. "I...well... uh...that...What's my name again?" he asked with a smile. Clearly, he felt it too.

I leaned in to kiss him back. "I forget, and I'm not sure what mine is either."

"Names are overrated," he said, reaching his arms around me. I think it was the creak of the dock that eventually brought us up for air. We had ended up leaning dangerously close to the edge of the dock, one inch away from falling into the water. We snapped back into normal time; sound, light, and other beings returned to our world once more.

"We almost fell in!" he exclaimed. "They should extend the railing here. Wait, what time is it?" he asked urgently, digging out his phone from his pocket.

"I have no idea."

He looked up from the phone. "It's five past six."

"OK, and..." I prompted, hurrying to catch up to him.

"I almost missed it," he said.

"What?"

"Paying attention—for posterity." He started typing something into his phone. "Our first kiss was on February fourteenth at five past six."

"You're writing that down?" I didn't understand what he was up to.

"Of course. So next Valentine's Day, we can come here on the anniversary of our first kiss, at exactly five past six, and mark the occasion." He stopped typing and raised his phone triumphantly. "Saved for posterity."

"It's Valentine's Day?" I asked obliviously.

"Why do you think I asked you to dinner *today*, for our first date?"

"I thought it was because it was Saturday and a weekend, when you weren't working. I haven't looked at a calendar in…weeks." He could see the surprise on my face, and he delighted in it.

"I wanted our first kiss to be on Valentine's Day, so we'd never forget the day. And it has to be said: that was an epic kiss."

How my heart continued to beat after it melted, I had no idea. I was falling for Sam so fast that gravity must have been jealous. "I still can't believe it's Valentine's Day," I said.

"It's a good thing you have me; otherwise you might have missed it. Before we go inside, I have to know: what were you thinking about when you melted the snow today?" Sam asked.

"Hmm, today? I can't really remember. It all happened so fast," I said lightly.

"You were thinking of *me*, weren't you?" he continued confidently.

"Like I said, I'm afraid I can't recall," I replied, of course, lying.

"It *was* me. That's fine if you won't tell me; you don't need to because I *know*. You're a terrible liar—*never* play poker. So all that time I spent shoveling your driveway and sidewalk, and hauling that snowplow over, and you could have just melted it with your mind!"

"Let's go inside," I said gently, taking his hand. We walked into the bright red building first built as a cannery in the 1890s, now restored and modernized into a coffee house, art gallery, and bistro. We were quickly taken to our table in the corner, under the soaring wood ceiling beams with a clear view of the water through the large, industrial windows. A guitarist strummed classical tracks near the fireplace. We talked about which of the photos on the wall were our favorite as we sat down at the table.

"I love this place," I said. "It's so cool what they've done with the building. Sam, how'd you become a chef? Did you go to culinary school? Oh! Do you think you could figure out how they cook the bistro's smoky macaroni and cheese? It's my absolute favorite. I don't even need to check the menu. That's what I always order here."

He laughed. "Smoky mac-and-cheese, huh? I'll see what I can do. No culinary school—as you know, I have three brothers. I'm the oldest of very rowdy boys, and our mom died very young."

"I'm sorry to hear about your mom," I said, reaching over for his hand.

"Thanks. She was amazing and dad just couldn't cope after she passed away. I chipped in to help my dad out and spent a lot of time cooking for everyone. Eventually, the kitchen became *my* room of the house, where I could be alone. As I started experimenting more with food, it was my favorite place to be. We couldn't afford college, and Dad needed help with the boys, so after high school I worked as a sous chef in a restaurant in Baltimore while living at home, and then eventually I worked as both a bartender and kitchen staff, learning along the way. It was tough, getting passed over for promotion by new chefs with degrees, but eventually I got the opportunity to be head chef. Now I own my restaurant, and it's been great. I don't know anything else. Besides, my brothers needed me. I still sometimes feel more like their dad than their brother."

"I often feel like Lou's mom, so I can relate to that. Did you ever want to do anything else?" I asked.

"For a long time I wanted to be an astronaut, but didn't we all? I think things work out the way they should. Remember, I believe in fate. So I'm happy as a chef. I guess it's what I'm supposed to be doing. Your turn. Did you go to art school?"

"No…and yes. I went to Western Washington University up in Bellingham. It was one of the few places I could find where they would support a biology degree along with art. I dual majored in biology and art studio. After that, I went to New York to an osteopathic med school in Harlem. Harlem is a terrific place to live, and the OD program was really cool, actually. My parents agreed that if I still wanted to pursue art after successfully completing my OD, then they would support me."

"What's an OD?" Sam asked.

"It's an osteopathic medical program, equivalent to an MD, meaning four years of med school. Osteopathic philosophy is that all the body's systems are interrelated, and it's important to understand the complexity as a whole," I explained.

"And it was your ticket to New York, a place to start in the art world. Mary was right; your parents had their hands full raising a coyote spirit," Sam joked.

"I don't disagree with that. I fought them on everything, but now that I look back on it, Mom was right to insist on med school, I guess. And it improved my art because I developed a good understanding of the human form. Portraits are my strong point. Science was always easy for me, but I enjoy art because it's such a challenge," I explained.

"Not only are you a medicine woman, but you're a real doctor too."

"I never took a state license board exam, but, yes, I completed med school, and I could be a doctor. Mom was surprisingly cool with the art choice, as long as I finished med school."

"I didn't realize that you were related to Lewis of 'Lewis and Clark.' The lighthouse was where Tamahna and Meriwether Lewis were married? I'm just putting together what Hannah told us and what we learned today from the tribe."

"Yes, recently my brother arranged for all us to get our DNA tested to prove the ancestry, and it's definitely true. We got the results just before mom and dad…Anyway, I haven't had time to deal with that. I grew up with the stories though. Meriwether fell for Tamahna very quickly—love at first sight. He was always exploring ahead of the corps, but after meeting her, he stayed put at Fort Clatsop, sending Clark out on *all* the excursions. They married within a day of meeting each other; of course, it was a different time."

"Love at first sight, huh? I can relate to that."

I tried to ignore the comment, albeit unsuccessfully by shifting nervously in my chair. "Meriwether once told her that when he looked up at the stars as a young man and imagined his future wife, he thought only of her, even though he didn't know it then."

"Something else I can relate to," Sam said.

My stomach turned in more knots, and I blushed. "This place is beautiful," I said. "Thanks for going with me today and for dinner out. It's been a great day."

"My pleasure," he replied, passing me a glass of wine. "So let's toast. Here's to us."

"Cheers," I said, thinking only about the moment, sitting across from Sam, toasting to us, on Valentine's Day. The perfection frightened me. For some reason, my mind drifted toward a tsunami on the Columbia River outside the window, moving like a skyscraper of black tar slowly in the moonlight, framed by the stars. Thinking about a tsunami then made me worry that I could cause one by thinking about it. My thoughts ran away from me.

Sam smiled and took another drink. He waved at the waiter. "I have a surprise for you. I e-mailed Martina at Carota Viola, and she sent me some recipes of your favorite dishes. The chef here is a friend of mine, so he was cool with that—chefs help each other out. I hope you don't mind that I planned the menu."

"Really?" I couldn't stop smiling.

"Yes, tonight you get your very own Carota Viola brought to you here in Astoria."

The waiter described our menu of saffron *arancini* as a starter, followed by rigatoni *ai carciofi*, and passion fruit *panna cotta* for dessert. Sam added a side of the smoky mac-and-cheese before the waiter left.

"And, by the way, Martina said that you'd be crazy not to fall for me," Sam added.

"She never said a word! I just talked to Martina last week, and she's terrible with secrets. I'm so surprised and—"

"Impressed?"

"Yes, very."

"Kay, being with you is…literally magical. I don't know how to explain it, but I'm sure that I was yours *before* we even met."

I looked at him and thought about the series of things that had brought us together, allowing us to find each other. He didn't say *soul mate*, but he seemed to mean it. Panic flowed across my mind. I felt as if this were a dream, and I was madly swimming against the current, afraid to float away with it, without knowing why. "What if this feeling is just a sort of keelalle spell or something, and you don't really feel that way about *me*—you're only in love with the idea of magic? I mean, we've only known each for what, three months?"

"Actually it's been one hundred and four days since we met, and I've contrived an excuse to see you at least once a day, only missing the week I went home for Christmas. How can you be worried that I'm in love with this *idea* of being with the medicine woman and not actually in love with the real you? We're twin souls. Have a little faith in…the universe."

I smiled, remembering how I had asked him if he spoke English. "How can this be real?"

"How about you just forget about being Dances-with-Coyotes for a while, and enjoy our very first date. Come on, Kay. We'll never have another *first* date."

"I'm sorry that I've been difficult, but I don't believe in signs. At least, I didn't. I don't know."

"I think the tribe is onto something with you being a coyote spirit. You're a lot like a coyote—independent, bold yet elusive, and a bit skittish. But that's OK. I get that about you. I'm not going anywhere. Take your time," he said gently. "Annette said that, as a dog spirit, my perfect match was a coyote spirit because I'm steady, faithful, and loyal. She said I'd have the patience to weather the coyote's uncertainty and independence. She was telling me about you, of course, but I didn't know it at the time."

"This scares me: you, me, all these mysterious keelalle things. Everyone I care about seems to disappear lately, and—"

"It scares you to get close, but you want to be close."

I closed my eyes for a minute. I needed to think. He waited. Adam would have plowed along, pushing me, but not Sam. Sam gave me time to catch my breath, allowing me to come up for fresh air. "Yes, exactly."

"You're right. That's the definition of skittish."

"Every day, Gran talks about my parents like they're around the corner, still alive. And sometimes when I'm pretending with her, I get caught up in it. Until I remember that they're gone, and then they're taken from me *again*...and again. Gran is *there,* and then she's gone too, sometimes within the same conversation. I feel like that person in those trust games, when you fall back and someone catches you, only every time I fall back, I hit the ground harder than the last time."

"I promise to catch you. I can see the future too, you know. It's not just a keelalle thing."

"Really? What does the future hold then?" I asked lightly.

He reached out to hold my hand. "Someday, I'm going to ask you to marry me, and you'll say yes," he said seriously. I forgot to breathe for a minute. I moved my hand back and pushed some stray hair back behind my ears.

"See…skittish," he confirmed.

"Ah—busted," I said with a laugh. "Sam, I'm not sure about soul mates, fate, coyote spirits, or controlling the weather, but I like being with you and I…want to be."

"That's good enough for now, amore mio," he said, leaning over to kiss me. Next we heard the chime of my cell phone. "Don't answer it, *please*."

"I have to—it could be Gran." I found the phone in my purse and saw that it was my home number. "Dorothy?"

"Kay! Kay!" Something crashed in the background and broke, which sounded like maybe a vase. "Kay, can you hear me?"

"Yes, I can hear…Is that glass? Are you OK?"

"I'm fine, but Hannah's in the kitchen throwing plates at me! She almost hit me. I had to run to the living room. I don't know what to do. She's *never* been like this, and she won't calm down."

"OK, OK, look, we're in Astoria, so we'll be there in about twenty minutes. Why don't you go home, OK? She'll be fine on her own for a short time. Let her calm down. Just watch the house from your window in case there's a fire or something. I'll be *right* there. I'm so sorry, Dorothy. You know that she doesn't mean it."

"I know, Kay. I'll go home now, but I'll keep an eye out from my window."

"Thanks. We're on our way." I hung up.

"I'll get the check. So much for a day off, huh?" Sam said, disappointed yet still supportive.

"I'm sorry—Gran's freaking out. She's screaming at Dorothy and throwing plates. This hasn't happened before. She's getting so much worse. Why can't I help her?"

"Don't apologize. You *are* helping her. Come on. Let's go."

"Lou will be here tomorrow, and he can help too. Rain check for dinner? I'm so sorry."

"Rain check, of course—that means a *second* date." Sam beamed.

"We should at least bring the food with us," I said.

"Don't worry. I'm a chef. I'll just make more tomorrow. You can come by the restaurant for lunch, or I'll bring it over to the house if you can't get away."

"You're terrific," I said appreciatively, as we hurried out.

"My pleasure," Sam said, placing his hand on my back. "Wait. Lou is coming—Lou is your brother, right? When is his flight getting in? Do you need me to pick him up from the airport?"

"I...uh...I don't know," I replied, realizing that I had no idea.

"So, you didn't talk to him...maybe you just *know* it? Like coyote-superpower know it?"

I couldn't remember how I knew it, but I was so confident. Sam was right. I had perceived the future somehow and almost didn't notice! "I guess you're not the only one who can see the future," I teased.

Outside at the motorcycle in the icy, snow-covered parking lot, Sam passed me a helmet, and I grabbed his hand. "Wait, Sam."

"Did you forget something?"

"Yes." I put my hand on the side of his face. "I forgot to say thank you." Then I leaned in to kiss him, and we stayed there for at least a minute.

Sam smiled and looked around, noticing how the snow in the whole parking lot had melted, leaving clear pavement. "You *were* thinking about me when you melted the snow! I *knew* it!" He smiled broadly and laughed.

Homecoming ❋

When we returned to the house, Dorothy met us in the driveway. She'd seen us arrive from her house across the street.

"I was watching through the window to make sure she didn't burn the house down or something," Dorothy said, panicked. "I don't know what happened, Kay. She just had some sort of mental break and started throwing plates at me."

I tried to calm her down. "It's not your fault, Dorothy. Don't worry. I'm here now. It will be OK."

"Kay, I hate to say this, but I think you need to start thinking about putting her in a home," Dorothy said.

"Never. Look, I have to go inside. Thanks again." Sam held onto my hand as I walked toward the door. Another voice called out to him.

"Sam, wait!" We turned around to see a young woman crossing the street from Dorothy's. "It's me, Rachel."

Sam let go of my hand, startled. He looked at me and leaned in close to whisper, "I'm sorry. I should have told you." Suddenly, I felt nervous.

"Rachel, what are you doing here?" Sam asked her.

"You asked me to marry you, and I'm saying yes," she said, pulling off her glove to show an engagement ring. "I wanted to surprise you for Valentine's Day. Surprised?"

The wind picked up, and snow started to fall in thick flurries; the temperature dropped significantly in a millisecond. I looked at Sam in shock, and I could barely breathe. "Your fiancée is standing in my driveway," was all I could say. At dinner, I had worried about a tsunami taking Sam away from me, and here it was, a fiancée tsunami, striking out of the blue. I heard things crashing in the kitchen of my house and quickly turned my attention to Gran, who was throwing something inside.

"Kay, this isn't—"

Something else broke inside the house. I had to deal with Gran first. The fiancée in the driveway would have to wait. I just couldn't believe it; it couldn't be true. "I can't...I have to go."

"Kay..." He squeezed my hand. I let go and ran inside.

I found Gran in the kitchen, standing by the sink and several opened cabinets. She was pulling out dishes from the cabinets and throwing them on the floor. Standing resolutely in her blue polka-dot pajamas, she added to the broken china on the floor. When she saw me, she looked at me blankly and said, "I have always hated this china set," as she threw another plate across the room—fortunately not in my direction.

My mind worked frantically to figure out if she was in a certain place and time, to try to track where she was. I didn't remember any story like this. "What's happening? What's wrong? Tell me."

"He's gone, and I couldn't save him. What do I need *twenty* place settings for anymore? It's only *me*, all alone."

I knew then what time she had traveled back to in her mind. She had to be remembering when Grandpa Charles had died in 1989. Poor thing—this all seemed so real to her.

"Dorothy didn't understand, Annette," she said, starting to calm down. "Kopet ikt lummieh. Do you know what that means?"

She was thinking I was Mom. Now I had to figure out how to play this out.

"Yes, Mother. Kopet ikt lummieh means "Only one old woman remains." But you aren't *alone*. We *all* miss Dad. There was nothing else that you could have done." She stopped and looked at me. "I never liked that china set either. Here, hand me a plate," I said. Why not? Maybe I'd just lost someone too, in my own driveway. Gran smiled and handed me a plate, and I threw it across the room at the refrigerator. It broke into at least twenty jagged pieces. "You're right. I do feel a little better," I said. "Let me get your shoes, though. Don't move—there's glass everywhere."

"OK, Annette. Then we'll start on the bowls," she said efficiently, as if we were working on a project together and checking off our lists for spring cleaning.

I went to the hallway to get her shoes so she wouldn't cut her feet on the shards of glass and china covering the kitchen floor. We finished destroying the bowls, and I was able to walk her to the living-room sofa where we sat down together as I checked to see if she had any cuts on her hands. Remarkably, she was fine, without a scratch.

"Are you going to put me in a nursing home, Kay?" she asked, clearly lucid.

"*Never*, Gran," I said, holding her hand. "Never."

"Thank you," she said simply. "I don't like old people." We laughed.

"I have good news. Lou's coming home tomorrow."

"He is? It will be so nice to see the boy. I've been waiting for him. I don't want to leave you alone," she said. The house shutters clicked against the house in the wind. "That's quite a sudden storm outside, my dear. What's wrong, child?"

"What do you mean?"

"Come on, Kehlok. I'm here *now*. I might be losing my mind, but I know when I'm *me*," she said. "At least, I *think* I do."

"Sam has a fiancée who's in the driveway, and I'm sad, angry, surprised, and confused. I don't know what to think. I can't believe it's true."

"Have a little faith in him. He's your twin soul. He belonged to you before you were born, like Charles belonged to me," she said. She smiled and added lightly, "Try not to take it out on the whole town with this storm. You must learn to control your power." Her hands smoothed over my hair, pushing some strays behind my ear.

"Why can't I heal *you*, Gran?"

"Probably for the same reason that I couldn't save Charles or your dear mother; we're not meant to. We can't stop the universe when it is someone's time to go to the spirit world. Not even Coyote could bring them back," she said. "I need you to remember that."

There was so much that I wanted to tell her, and I didn't know how long the window of lucidity would remain. I spoke quickly. "I met the tribe today, in Seaside. John Lane Junior is the chief, and he's a raven." I knew that she'd be happy to hear that.

Gran smiled. "Little Johnny Lane? Isn't that something. A raven *and* a coyote? Just as the legends said. He's like you, so modern and yet such an old soul—and stubborn. He'll take care of you. I don't have to worry so much now," she said, sounding relieved. "You have Sam, Lou, and little Johnny Lane. You will not be alone."

"I'm not alone because I have *you*," I replied. I had to ask about the journals. "Gran, where are the journals? You know, Meriwether Lewis's journals, the copies he gave to Tamahna. Where are they?"

"My dear, you already know." Her eyes changed, and I knew instantly she was lost again, a prisoner in her own mind. I'd learned to recognize the look by now. "Ask your mother when she's back from work today. She'll tell you," Gran said, once again lost to me but not lost. "Oh my word, that's a terrible storm outside. Listen to that wind. Such strange weather we're having this summer. Imagine, snow in July!"

My face fell. There was never enough time with *her*. "It's late. Why don't we get upstairs and get you into bed?" I asked gently, standing up and reaching out my hand.

"I am feeling very tired," she said.

"Me too," I agreed. "Me too."

"Why are all these broken dishes on the floor?" she asked, both alarmed and shocked.

I couldn't help but laugh. "It was an earthquake," I replied quickly. "I'll clean it up. Don't worry."

"I hope that doesn't mean a flood is coming. Saghalie held the tsunami back. She heard it first before the first quake...the roar of the great wave." She started to sing, "She heard the roar 'fore the quake."

"Saghalie turned the power of the sea," I finished.

"Saghalie turned the power of the sea," she returned. "You must know the sound when you hear it, Kehlok—the roar before the quake."

She wasn't making any sense. Still, I agreed to validate her. "Yes, Gran, I will know. Come on. Off to bed now. It's late."

She squeezed my hand tightly and looked into my eyes. I saw the flash of recognition. "You must know the sound, Kehlok—the roar of the waves before the quake. You must know it." Her eyes darted behind me as if she saw someone standing behind me. "I'm very tired, dear. Charles is waiting for me upstairs."

"OK, come on. It's time for bed," I repeated.

We walked upstairs, and I waited for her to fall asleep, feeling unsettled by the scene earlier and thinking about our conversation. Once she started snoring, I slipped away downstairs to clean up the mess in the kitchen. After gathering up the broken remains of our kitchen place settings into some cardboard boxes, I surveyed what we did have left. We still had the teacups and saucers, but the other cupboards were bare. Gran had destroyed all the plates, coffee cups, bowls, and glasses.

I left the boxes in the kitchen, figuring that Louis could somehow lift them into the garbage bins later. I also took in more wood for the fire, as the house felt so cold. I put on a sweater and even grabbed a scarf from the hall. The teapot whistled, and I made a cup to warm up and took advantage of the quiet time. I wanted to be mad about Rachel, but something in my mind wouldn't let me. Lou would be here soon, and I'd deal with Sam later.

An hour later, there was a knock on the door, and I checked my watch to realize it was one o'clock in the morning already. I wondered why Sam hadn't come over yet. Then I hustled toward the door, excited to discover Louis standing there in the snow with his luggage.

"Come in, come in!" I said excitedly, giving him a big hug first before helping him with his luggage. "I've been waiting for you all night. It's good to see you. You look good, Lou."

"Hey, Sis, it's good to be home. Took me *ages* to get here. The roads were terrible; the storm has pushed trees down in the road in places. Since when do we get *feet* of snow in Ilwaco? But wait a minute—I didn't call. I wanted to *surprise* you, so how did you…" Louis stammered as he stepped inside.

"The short answer is that I now have some inexplicable keelalle ways, evidently including being able to *know* things like Mom and also…to change the weather," I said evenly.

"OK…um…We're going to circle back to…that weather thing, but first, why is it like a thousand degrees inside this house?" he asked.

"What do you mean? It's *freezing* in here. I just made some tea," I said, still shivering.

"No, Kay, it's a *sweat lodge* in here," he said, taking off his jacket and sweater, leaving only a T-shirt and jeans. "Are you feeling OK? Look at the thermostat—it's seventy-nine degrees!" He opened the kitchen window.

And then I knew: death was closing in. "It's Gran. We're losing her! Come on. She's upstairs. Hurry!" Louis followed me as I bounded upstairs to Gran's room, where she lay very still, struggling to breathe. I woke her up, checked her pulse, and dialed 911.

"Gran! Wake up. Wake up. Lou's here. He's *here*," I said, holding her hand and frantically thinking, trying to determine whether there was anything we could do. We helped her sit, moving the pillows to prop her up.

"Hello? Nine-one-one? Please send an ambulance to six-one-two Cedar…It's my grandmother, presenting with short-ness of breath and acute coronary…Dear God, please hurry," I said, feeling death's chill advancing by the second. It was hap-pening too fast; they would never get here in time. Her hands felt clammy, and her pulse was far too slow and erratic. Why couldn't I have "seen" this if I could see the future?

"No, Kehlok, it's my time," said Gran. "No doctors, besides…They can't help me now, and you *know* that."

"Why couldn't I see this coming?" I asked desperately. I knew she had minutes left. Her body was failing fast.

"Your powers are still very new, and it takes *great* strength to see what you do not want to see. Meriwether, my dear boy, you are *here*. You are so much like your grandfather, always out seeking adventure, so brave and strong."

"Gran...Kay, do *something*!" Louis urged.

"Meriwether," Gran continued, "you need to know how much I love you...and how much your parents loved you."

I touched her cheek gently, still holding her hand tightly with my other hand. Louis held her other hand. "We love you, Gran. Please don't go. Don't leave us alone," I pleaded, feeling helpless. Tears ran down my face.

"You are not *alone*, Kehlok. I see Charles again, waiting for me in the veil," she said, staring past us into the world beyond. "And Annette and Henry—oh, they are smiling." She coughed and wheezed, struggling for breath. "Let me go, Kehlok. Let go of my hand."

I let go and then she was gone. Louis looked at me with pain in his eyes as he struggled to be strong and not cry. I reached out for his hand, my eyes blurry with tears. "No... no...I just..." he faltered.

"It's OK to cry," I told him, which is what I knew he needed me to say. We both cried together, now orphaned while everyone else in our family joined together in another world. We stayed in the room with her, waiting for the grief to numb us and allow us to function.

When the ambulance arrived, Lou met them at the door. I couldn't leave her alone, even though she was gone. Sam rushed over when he saw the flashing lights of the ambulance and stood with us, holding my hand as we watched them carry her away. He walked us back into the house.

"I don't know about you, Kay, but I could use a drink," Louis said.

"Me too—there's some Scotch above the fridge," I said.

Sam stood up quickly. "I'll get it. You two should sit down." Sam returned a few minutes later with two teacups and a bottle of Scotch. "What happened to all the glasses? This was all I could find," he said, concerned, as he passed me a teacup of Scotch.

I laughed through my tears and told them what had happened. There was a knock at the door. I jumped up quickly to answer it. John stood on the porch, and I was surprised to see him.

"I got here as soon as I could," John said. "How's Hannah?"

"But how could you have known? She's gone." I stared at him in disbelief as we walked into the living room.

"Nice of you to come over, brother," Sam said.

"The crazy thing is Kay didn't actually call me—it's the coyote-raven hotline," John explained. "I was asleep, and I heard her talking to nine-one-one like she'd called me. It was so strange, but the good news is that we're linked!"

"Maybe sort that out later, man...Hannah..." Sam reminded gently.

"Right, sorry. Is that Scotch in a tea cup?" John's gaze stopped at Louis. "You must be Louis, I'm John. I'm very sorry for your loss. Hannah was a kind woman."

"Coyote-raven hotline?" Lou repeated, confused.

"I don't believe it," I muttered. "That's...impossible."

"Who are you guys anyway? Why are you here?" Lou asked.

John answered quickly, bringing Lou up to speed. "That's Sam—the neighbor and our newest Clatsop tribe member and Kehlok's twin soul. I'm John, the chairman of the Clatsop-Nehalem tribal council."

Lou's forehead wrinkled as he narrowed his eyes, looking at me expectantly. I drank some Scotch before trying to explain. "Lou, I told you about the council meeting I went to, remember?"

"Yeah, but I guess I just didn't believe it." Lou shrugged his shoulders.

"Neither did I then really...but all these things and...Sam. I'm evidently the real deal of super keelalles."

"So Sam's like your soul mate? And you're some sort of magical healer now who can change the weather? And we're all having this conversation now, right after Gran...I mean if you are this special keelalle, why couldn't you help her? This is absurd, Kay, even for you." It was Lou's turn to finish off his Scotch. Sam and John froze.

Lou's words stung me, and I remembered Rachel standing in the driveway. My mind flashed to Gran's eyes closing for the last time. I looked at John, sitting on our sofa after the centuries-old keelalle-and-chief hotline was reestablished. Only hours ago I was willing to believe in the magic of twin souls and coming into my keelalle ways, but in that moment I didn't want any more of it. I felt a darkness set in, combined of anger, resentment, and grief. Thunder boomed outside, and we all heard a loud crack.

"Was that a tree?" John asked, rushing to look outside.

"A tree fell down in the backyard...I'm very upset," I explained as my heart pounded. "Sam's fiancée...Gran...I just...everything and I can't breathe." Thunder cracked again, so loudly a vase fell off a shelf in the living room.

"Kehlok, you need to calm down," John said. He then scowled over at Sam, noting, "A *fiancée*? Really?"

Sam sighed. "If Kay would *talk* to me about this, then she would know. Kay, let me explain about Rachel—"

"Gran died!" Another loud crack from a tree falling. My emotions were all over the map.

Lou jumped at the noise. "Damn! That one almost hit the *house*!"

"Kay, I know that you're upset right now, but don't take it out on the whole town, kitten," Sam said, calmly walking toward me and with each step somehow making me feel more calm.

"I don't know what's more strange—that you let the neighbor here into the tribe after refusing to let my dad in because he was Chinook, or that you two seem to think that my sister controls the weather," said Lou.

"Lou, you missed a lot, man. Don't interrupt. Let us handle this," John said evenly.

"Don't tell my brother what to do, John!" I yelled. A flash of lightning lit up the yard outside.

John stood up. "Kehlok, I'm the chief, and you are my keelalle. If you don't calm down, you're going to destroy...possibly the Western Seaboard. It's been a long night, and we're all tired. So we should all just relax, get some sleep, and deal with this in the morning."

"I'm *not* a child. Don't tell me what to do!" I stood my ground firmly, as the wind outside nearly ripped the shutters from the windows.

John looked knowingly at Sam, who moved steadily toward me. "Sam…your turn."

"Kay, I'm going to try this out. Please don't hit me with a bolt of lightning." He reached out to touch my face. "I think we need to hug this out."

I pushed him in a slight protest, only to melt into him the second his arms were around me. "That's not fair! I really want to be mad at you right now." The wind died down, and it seemed as if suddenly the storm had passed.

"I know. It's a dirty trick. If it makes you feel any better, I kind of wanted to be mad at you too for doubting me, but all I want to do now is kiss you." And I let him. "You really should get some rest, amore mio. We'll talk in the morning, OK?"

"OK," I agreed quietly, feeling utterly exhausted and turning around to walk upstairs as Sam followed closely, not letting go. I fell into the bed, too tired to think about anything, even Gran. Sam sat down beside me.

"Do you want to talk about it?" he asked quietly.

I didn't. "No."

"Do you want me to leave?" he asked.

I was desperate for him to stay. "No," I repeated.

"OK, then I'll stay." He lay down beside me, and I fell asleep in his arms.

To the Lighthouse ❁

J woke up with a start over six hours later, sometime around nine o'clock, startled to discover Sam wasn't there. I'd had a nightmare that I was drowning, tossed beneath massive waves of water. When I woke, I gasped for air. I didn't want to fall back to sleep, so I got up and dressed quickly. Down the hall, I found Louis snoring peacefully and knew only too well that he'd be asleep for another several hours. Having adapted to Gran's strange sleep schedule, I felt fine with the five hours of sleep. I looked into her room and saw that the bedding had been removed, and some things had been boxed up. I heard voices and activity in the kitchen and soon discovered John and Mary drinking coffee and sitting at the table, eating croissants.

"Good morning," I said, walking toward the coffee pot.

Mary stood up and intercepted me with a big hug. "Good morning, dear. I'm so sorry to hear about Hannah. She was a good woman," she said, pulling me close. "Sit down and let me get you some coffee and breakfast. We're here to take care of you."

I obeyed, sitting down next to John. "When did you get here, Mary?" I asked, still surprised to see her at my house.

"John called last night. I left Seaside around six o'clock this morning. Here you are," she said, passing me a cup of coffee and a plate with fresh croissants.

"Thank you. Where did these plates come from?"

"Sam got them and the other dishes from his restaurant sometime after you went to sleep. You have a whole set again. Of course, he also made the croissants at the restaurant while he was gathering the dishes. Good, aren't they?" Mary asked.

"Not *good*—incredible," John replied.

"Sam was here all night?" I asked.

John answered, "Yeah, after you went to sleep, he started boxing up things in Hannah's room so you wouldn't have to face it all this morning. Once he finished with that, he got the dishes from the restaurant and made these amazing things. Seriously, I've already had like four."

"Where is he now?" I asked, feeling disoriented.

"Across the street at Dorothy's, and he's been over there since about eight. She was so upset this morning, so he brought her some croissants. We didn't think that you would be awake for another few hours," John explained.

"And his fiancée? What did he say about her showing up last night? Is she at Dorothy's too?" I allowed myself to be insecure and grumpy.

John and Mary exchanged a knowing look, but Mary responded. "He said that he shouldn't have to tell you what you already know."

"What's that supposed to mean?" I asked angrily.

Mary sighed. "John told him that you weren't ready."

I looked at John, annoyed. "Ready for what?"

John shook his head. "Kehlok, this is hard for him too. I can't tell you. I've promised. Besides we have a bet. These croissants are delicious. Does he cater?"

Mary shook her head at John and sat down next to me. "Kehlok, you must listen to your heart for the answers you seek. A keelalle's power comes from love, and you cannot live halfway as a keelalle. It is time to embrace your destiny or choose another path."

"That's right, Kehlok. It's time to choose where you will stand; a sequoia's strength comes from its roots. If you leave Clatstop lands, then the magic leave with you."

I focused on my coffee cup as if I were reading tea leaves—or in this case, the grounds. "I need to get some air," I said, standing up and taking the coffee cup with me. "Thank you for being here. Can you stay here with Lou? I don't want him to be alone."

John quickly agreed. "Of course. You're family now. We're here as long as you need. Betty, James, and Earl will be here later this afternoon. They are bringing more food. Do you need anything else?"

"Thank you. I'm very grateful. All I need is someone to be there for Lou. He knows where I'll be." I found the car keys and left the house. I stood in the driveway for an entire minute, thinking about walking over to Dorothy's. I wanted to see Sam, but then I wasn't sure. I didn't know what any of it meant. I took about twenty steps toward Dorothy's and then stopped in the middle of the street.

I stood there for a minute, sipped my coffee, and then walked ten steps back toward the car before stopping short again. Turning to face Dorothy's house, I stood with my coffee for a few minutes and then paced a bit in circles. I wanted to go to Sam and to know that Rachel was on a flight back to wherever she'd come from. But then what? Live with him in my parents' house, stuck in this town forever as super keelalle? Or haul him to New York and sever my relationship with the tribe? What was I doing? What did I actually *want*? I didn't know. I took a deep breath, went back to the car, and drove away.

I went to the lighthouse and sat on a bench nearby, overlooking the sea cliff, as I watched the icy fog roll away from the coast. The veil between worlds was thin there, and I could feel it. I felt both my mother's and grandmother's spirits there, as well as their compassion. I suddenly felt stronger. Where the veil between worlds was thin, those paying attention could connect with the other side, like hearing a waterfall but not seeing it. My thoughts resembled the icy fog hugging the beach—opaque.

The rain didn't bother me, and neither did the cold. It was how I felt inside, and it seemed natural to have that reflected in the weather outside. I cried a little, and the rain washed away my tears. I didn't know how long I sat there; time seemed to fade away as I breathed in the ocean air. I came to the veil to decide. I came for answers.

In New York, I chose where I lived, who I was with, and where I worked, but here nothing felt like anything that I chose. I lived in my parents' house, one they'd inherited that had been in my family since it was built in 1891. The furniture was beautiful, but nothing I'd selected and purchased. I'd inherited my parents' friends in the neighborhood, as all of mine had moved away, minus Kristin, who still lived in Astoria.

Even Sam had been *sent* to me. I hadn't spotted him in a bar and walked up to him or bumped into him in a shop and talked to him. I hadn't chosen to be a keelalle, let alone one destined to be the most powerful in ten generations. My life was not my own, yet it very much was.

With Gran gone, I could return to New York. I could return to all of my choices and own them all, regardless of fate. Today I was *free*. Every door had been opened to me, and all that was left was the decision to stay here or go. Mary was right; I could not live halfway as a keelalle. John was right too; I could only be a keelalle here in this place.

I needed to be certain. I waited for some sort of sign or feeling, ironically wanting the universe to tell me what to do, instantly realizing that it already had spoken so clearly. In my mind, my thoughts flashed back to the *Motorcycle Man* paintings and then quickly ahead. I could see myself laughing at a big party in the house, which was a wedding party on a sunny day. My daughter smiled at me as Sam walked her down the aisle. I saw Sam and me, much later, with gray hair, walking along the beach holding hands. The more I thought about everything, the more I realized that I had missed the point. Most people spend their life-time searching for their soul mate, where I was lucky enough for him to be given directions and practically arriving with a "Hey, lady, I'm your twin soul and totally cool with that" neon T-shirt.

I'd been so busy running and taking care of everyone else that I couldn't see the big picture. I had run away to New York, but now I was home. My place in this world was *this* place.

Sam would go with me anywhere, but this was where we both belonged. I was the keelalle. My place was with my tribe here at the veil.

Suddenly, everything made sense to me. I felt lighter and more liberated than I had in a long time. As I watched a seagull fly above the fog, I felt like a sequoia growing tall above the land, leveraging its deep roots. This was my home. This was my choice. Instantly, I felt powerful, as if I could fly.

I closed my eyes and smiled. He was coming for me, meeting me halfway. Sam knew that I needed the time to choose and catch up to him, forging my own path. The gale that was a cool sea breeze seemed to suddenly warm enough for me to notice, but not enough for me to take my hands out of the warm coat pockets. The rain cleared, and the fog moved out sea. Remaining still, I took a deep breath and heard him sit down next to me—*my* Sam. I knew without looking that he was beside me, yet I continued staring at the green rolling ocean waves below.

"Louis told me that I'd find you here," he said simply. "I saw you on the street. You *almost* made it over. We were rooting for you. I bet John ten dollars that you'd go find me at Dorothy's to talk. I would have met you in the street, but I could see that you needed some time to think. So? Have you decided? With Hannah having passed, you are free. You don't have to stay here or be super keelalle. You can live anywhere. Just know that I will follow. Uh…that was meant to sound romantic, but it came out kind of stalker-ish."

I nodded in agreement. "Yes, I'm as free as those birds." I continued to watch the birds and the water. "Imagine growing up with people telling you that you were going to be the next Santa Claus. And then your parents die, and elves pick you up in a sleigh and fly you to the North Pole. It's unbelievable. And I've been struggling with it."

"You're related to Santa Claus too? Cool. Our kids will get awesome presents," he joked.

"No, I'm trying to explain why this has been so difficult for me. If I believe in one small part of it, then I have to believe in *all* of it—the elves, the flying reindeer, or, in my case, the talking coyotes, tsunamis, controlling the weather, and twin souls. All of a sudden, all those legends are not stories but *history*. If I believe in you as my twin soul, then I have to believe in everything else too. I can't pick and choose."

"Where for me, it's a cool story and magical, but for you it's responsibility and a whole destiny thing," he said thoughtfully.

"I don't know how to be a super keelalle, or what that even means. I'm still figuring things out. And this morning, I decided to stop fighting it. I'm a super keelalle who can heal people, change the weather, and occasionally see the future. My place is here…with you."

"Of course, I sent Rachel home, back to New York, but you already know that. What you don't know is that I proposed to her last year, and we were going to move to New York together, but then she started seeing someone else. I guess the guy broke up with her, and she figured that maybe we could get back together, but I set her straight. Well?"

"I did know, not the details, but I knew it wasn't real—that you were mine, not hers. Thank you for giving me the time I needed."

"Anytime." He put his arm around my shoulders, and I leaned into him.

"We'll be happy here," I said. I closed my eyes and breathed in his scent. I could hear him smile. He kissed my hair and pulled me closer.

"I brought you these," he said, holding up a small bouquet of snowdrops. "I picked them on the way up here. I'm so sorry about Hannah."

"Thank you. They are beautiful. What happened to you?" I asked, finally looking over at him and seeing that he was caked in mud, his hair askew. There were some small scrapes on his face and hands. He looked as if he'd had to fight his way here, through some sort of muddy boot-camp obstacle course. I covered a smirk with my hand.

"That trail is a *nightmare* in this weather! I've only been out here in the summer. It took me an *hour* to walk over from the visitor center on that so-called fifteen-minute path. I fell *four* times on the ice, slid right into some mud patches, and nearly fell into the ocean *twice*. Dead Man's Cove almost got another victim. I cut my hand on a branch when I fell the last time. How is it that you're not a mess too?" he asked.

"I parked at the bottom of the road, by the coast guard station," I said, trying desperately not to laugh.

"Ah...well...I didn't know that people could park there. I've only been up in the summer," he said, clearly chagrined. "But this is how *chivalrous* I am: I would have walked through that punishing mud trail *twelve* times to find *you* on the other side of it."

"I can wait here if you want another crack at it," I teased, happy in his arms.

Sam smirked. "I prefer the view from here," he said, pulling me closer to him as he leaned in to kiss me.

My stomach turned in knots, and I didn't care at all about anything else in the world. I sighed and caught my breath. I reached for his hand, found the cut, and kissed it. Instantly it healed and disappeared.

"Wow, that's a new one. Literally 'kiss and make it better,'" he said simply. "Looks like it never happened!"

"Well, I'm super keelalle now, remember?" I whispered. He took off his scarf and wrapped it around me, kissing me on the cheek.

"Why are we up here again?" he asked.

"I wanted to be near Gran and Mom. They happened to build the lighthouse at the veil—you see, keelalles have always lived here because the veil between worlds is thin on this high cliff above the ocean, at the end of the world. This cape is one of the many sacred places where the spirit world touches our world, like Iona, Scotland; or Varanasi, India; or Stonehenge. Gran always said that Tamahna told Lewis that she'd meet him at the end of the world, and this is where she waited. Even though most of the tribe lived near what is Seaside today, keelalles always lived here, in the shadow of the veil."

"I love you, Kay Baker, and I don't care if that scares the hell out of you or if you're ready to hear it. I love you. And I'll gladly sit here all day, just to be with you. I knew it that first day we met. Remember how speechless I was? I had no idea that love at first sight would knock the wind out of me." He held my hand and looked at me while I gazed toward the ocean. I still needed a second, and he obliged.

We sat silently, watching the waves retreat from the beach with the tide. I closed my eyes to listen to the in-between. In that easy silence, I found my words. "I love you," I finally said quietly.

"I know, amore mio. Still, it's nice to hear you say it," Sam replied. "Wow! This is a big step for us—yesterday our first kiss and today you finally realized that I'm the love of your life." He laughed with a shameless certainty that was only his.

"You're right," I said. "What are we going to do tomorrow to top that?" I smiled.

"I can think of at least one or two things," he said with a twinkle in his eye.

I rested my head on his shoulder, and we remained still for a while. I didn't know how long, actually, but we sat quietly watching the waves and distant fog.

"I feel a little guilty," I confessed. "I'm so happy with you here, right now, and we just lost Gran. I should feel sad, shouldn't I?"

"She wanted you to be happy," he said. "Grief is strange; it ebbs and flows. When my mom died, my dad fell apart, and he was unable to cope for almost five years. I held it together, even though I was a kid. Someone had to get my brothers dressed, fed, and off to school. Eventually my dad started to return to himself, and we all seemed OK. Then one day, I opened his closet to borrow a tie for a school dance, and I saw all her clothes still there. It hit me hard, only then. And it took me a long time after that to come to terms with the loss and to allow myself to be happy. Still, I haven't worn a tie since then."

"That's why you swooped in last night to clear out her room," I noted.

"Crying now or later doesn't mean that you loved her any less. You loved her and allowed her to keep her dignity to the very end. The love is what's important, Kay. Nothing else matters."

"I will never ask you to wear a tie," I said with tears in my eyes.

Eventually we heard footsteps crunching on the snow. John appeared with blankets, an umbrella, and two cups of coffee. He smiled. "We started to get worried. Louis sent me out here to check on you. It's been hours since anyone has seen either one of you. Thought you could use these," he said, handing over the blanket and coffees. "Hey, brother, you owe me ten bucks. What happened to you, man? You look like a Sasquatch made of mud."

"I didn't know you could park at the bottom of the hill," Sam replied. "Hand me that blanket."

John laughed. "My dad always parked down there. He didn't like the trail. I haven't been up here since his ashes ceremony after the funeral. Kehlok, it is cold up here. Why don't you warm things up? Come on. Let's see it," he said, sitting down next to us.

"I shouldn't," I protested.

"I'm freezing here, girl, and I might have lost feeling in my toes," Sam said with a laugh.

I closed my eyes and thought about all the love that surrounded me, how Sam had trudged through the mud and stayed up all night, how John and the tribe had stepped in as family, and how Gran had been able to pass with dignity on her own terms, with me and Lou beside her. There was so much love around. "That's better," Sam said, pulling me closer to him and kissing my cheek.

"Oh, Sam! Good news, brother," John announced. "The tribe came up with a real native name for you: Bebe Talapus," he said with a grin from ear to ear.

"Rock on, I have my own native name! Let me guess: it means 'Handsome Devil'?" Sam asked brightly.

"No, it means 'man who kisses coyotes.'" John laughed and I joined him. Sam shook his head.

"Well, as long as the coyote in question is this girl here, then you can call me whatever you want," Sam said as he leaned in to kiss me. I forgot John was there for a few seconds until I heard him stand up and clear his throat to remind us of his presence.

"I'll head back then and let Louis know you're both fine. You brought her flowers too…nice touch, Bebe Talapus," John said. I looked again at the flowers and thought of Gran and Mom.

"Picked them myself too, on the way here," Sam said proudly.

"As you were crawling through the mud?" John asked flippantly.

"Anything for my girl," Sam said like a veteran from a war.

More Secrets ✤

ary and Sam stepped in quickly to help arrange Gran's funeral, only occasionally asking for input, like the type of flowers or music. Lou and I spent our time going through the house and clearing out Mom and Dad's room. It was a difficult time, but I didn't want to do it myself and possibly risk giving something away that Lou really wanted. We started in their room, knowing it would the hardest.

"Remember these?" Lou asked, holding up a bright red pair of trousers my dad had in his closet. "Mom hated them."

I smiled. "He thought they looked European. I thought she gave those away years ago."

"They were mashed up here, way in the back. I guess he wanted to hold onto them for that next big family trip to Europe that we never took. We only went to Scotland, in August."

"Yeah, no one told us about all the mosquitos, but they weren't too bad out on the island. I remember that your face was red from mosquito bites. Gosh, we were little then. I was—what?—seven? So you must have been five."

"That was our only trip to Europe. Dad wanted to see Paris, but Mom said she couldn't leave the veil, and eventually Iona was the compromise."

"I remember that they call mosquitos 'midges' in Scotland, and everywhere we went, you kept telling people that you were attacked by *midgets*. It was so funny. And Dad wore those red trousers like every day." I laughed, remembering us playing on the beach, when the water was still subzero in August, Dad in his silly red trousers and Mom fussing about Lou's face.

Lou laughed. "Yeah, and Mom kept putting some sort of kelp mash on my face, trying to make the big red blotches go away. I looked like a sea monster." He smiled at me and looked again at the red trousers. "I think I'll keep these," he said simply.

"OK, you should." I took a deep breath, smiled, and wiped a tear from the corner of my eye.

"I'm sorry that I missed their funeral," he said.

"It's OK. You were at sea."

"Still…"

"Let's keep sorting. I feel like I can only get through this because you're here. This room…this house…has been a museum. It had to be for Gran, as any changes made her more unstable."

"Will you be selling the place? I mean, you could if you wanted to move back to New York," Lou noted.

"No. I won't be selling or going to New York. This is our *home*. I have no idea what I'm going to do with a four-bedroom house, but I can't leave. Finally, I understand what Mom was saying about the veil and why she couldn't leave the cape. I felt it this morning."

"Good. I'm glad you'll be staying here. I would miss this place."

"You'll always have your room here, Lou," I said.

"So, that Sam…You gonna tell me about him? Is he the reason you're suddenly all fine about living in Ilwaco?"

I smiled. Strangely, my mind flashed to seeing Louis with a pregnant woman, while he carried a large brown moving box into their house. "Wait—did you get married and she's pregnant?" I said loudly, shocked. Lou's face dropped and he looked stunned, like he did every Christmas as a kid when Santa magically knew his name.

He narrowed his eyes. "Fine…I got married, OK? There! Are you happy now? Her name is Ashley, and we met last year at a concert. We got married right after Mom and Dad died. That's why I couldn't move up here."

I almost couldn't believe it, but then again, this was exactly my little brother's style of operating. "So you've been married for *three* months, and this is the *first* I've heard of it? Meriwether Louis, you little—"

Thunder clapped above the roof, shaking the house a little, and footsteps on the stairs soon followed. Lou looked like he'd seen a ghost, his face was so pale. Thunder had terrified him as a child, and now his sister seemed to control it. I knew I had to tone it down.

Mary, John, and Sam spilled into the room. "What's going on up here?" John asked expectantly. "Sam, maybe you should—"

Sam nodded and stepped over toward me, making a bee-line to calm any outburst. He smelled of whatever that pine tree, ocean-scented aftershave was, intoxicating me for a second that I stopped to catch my breath. He was so handsome. Still, I raised my hand for him to stop.

"Just go back downstairs. I need a minute with my brother. We're only *talking*. I'll calm down," I said reassuringly.

Sam looked at Lou and then back at me. "Play nice, kitten," he said simply. "Go easy on the boy. Come on. Let's give them some space. Nothing to see here, folks." They left, although they most likely remained lurking around, trying to eavesdrop.

"Sorry, I'm just learning how to control this...whatever it is. It's tied into my emotions, and I'm still figuring out how to separate them from my keelalle powers."

"Uh...OK. I don't know that I believe any of this yet, but there is an eerie coincidence with you being angry and all hell breaking loose."

"I promise not to electrocute you. Now, why didn't you tell me?" I demanded.

"Look, I was feeling bad about not being at the funeral because I was at sea, and Ashley decided to cheer me up with a weekend trip to Vegas after I got home. We went to spend time together and forget the real world, and...we kind of ended up getting married."

"You got married in Vegas by accident?" I started laughing so hard that tears were in my eyes. "My little brother, the soldier and workaholic who planned *everything* in his life, got married on a whim in Vegas?" I took a deep breath.

"I wanted to tell you, but you were so stressed out with Gran and this house, and then I flaked on not coming here."

"And then you missed Christmas," I continued.

"By Christmas I felt *really* bad, and we went to Ashley's parents' house in Tucson. The longer I waited to tell you, the worse it got. She can't move because of her job, and then... I'm getting out of the navy this summer, so I won't be gone as much. I didn't want to tell you this on the phone, so I waited. I'm sorry, Kay. But, well...I'm going to want to be home more often now that we're married. I have a good job offer from SeaWorld, so I'll still be working in the water, but I'll be home for dinner every night. She's a realtor in San Diego, and moving now would mean a huge drop in income while she built her brand up somewhere else."

"And the baby?" I took a deep breath. This was already a lot to take in while I also focused on staying calm to avoid any thunder and lightning. After last night's episode, the backyard already looked like drunk loggers had conquered it. I wished Mom were here to help me with this. Still, Mom probably wouldn't have had any idea what to do either, as I was the first of our family in ten generations to have these capabilities. There was no guide out there to help me.

"Yes, she's pregnant, five months now—also a factor in us getting married."

"Mom must have known," I said.

"Of course she did. She called me the day we found out. It's a boy, by the way. We're going to name him after Dad."

I nodded in agreement and leaned over to hug him. "He'd like that," I said simply. "Wow, so is *that* everything now? Am I all caught up? I don't think I can take any more surprises."

Lou laughed. "Yeah, you're all caught up now. Are you still mad?"

"No, I'm not mad. I get that you didn't want to tell me over the phone, and I was spinning around Gran and moving back here."

"So we're good?" he asked.

"Yeah, we're good. You can come inside now, Sam. I know you're lurking," I said loudly.

Sam poked his head out into the doorframe. "Sorry, I just stayed to look after Lou, you know, in case you electrocuted him or something.

"Congratulations, man," Sam said, walking over to shake Lou's hand. "So, San Diego, huh? Maybe when we visit, we'll catch a Padres game. What do you think, Kay? We could go down there when the baby's born?"

Typical Sam—making everything normal and easy. I grinned, happy to see them getting along. "Yes, that's a good idea. We should be there for that."

Lou beamed. "We'll have plenty of room for you to stay. Ashley found a three-bedroom townhouse, and we're closing on it this month. She said that I had to tell you *everything* before we bought the place, and that would be one more thing we hadn't told you."

"Thank her for that from me," I said. "And you're going to need furniture for that new house of yours. Pick out whatever you want, and you can drive it back in a truck. We'll rent one this week. You should get back to your family after Gran's funeral."

He nodded. "Thanks, Kay. I've felt terrible not telling you about this."

"I know. I knew there was something, but I didn't know what it was. Don't worry about it. We'll come down in May when the baby's born."

"But he's not due until the end of June."

I nodded. "Like I said, we'll visit in *May* when the baby's born."

Sam chuckled and under his breath whispered, "Super keelalle ways."

Lou laughed along with him, and his eyes were wide open. "The baby's coming early?" he said nervously.

"He'll be fine. Don't worry. He's merely got his father's timing," I said.

With everyone's help, we soon cleared out the bedrooms and filled the garage with boxes and furniture that Lou would take with him to San Diego. I also gained space to personalize the house myself, and I felt lighter about the house not being a museum anymore. I could make it my own now, and Lou had everything he needed to make a fresh start.

Before Lou and John loaded up the rental truck with furniture, I escaped to Sam's.

"What a terrific surprise," he said, leaning in for a kiss. "I was just about to go over and see if they needed help with the truck."

"Lou and John are packing up the furniture and things Lou wanted, and I decided it would be best if I wasn't there. I don't want him to feel like he has to run everything by me first. I've already got the house, car, and the clinic from the will," I explained.

"Come on in, darling. Want some wine? I have a terrific pinot from that Yakima vineyard that I know you'll enjoy."

"Yes, please," I replied. I spotted some laundry on the living-room floor, and Sam followed my gaze. "Oh, that's not me. Neb misses me when I'm at work, and she's started bringing my clothes downstairs in protest. First it was the shoes, and then she managed to pull open the drawers and get to the T-shirts. She's starting her own Occupy movement in the living room."

"Sure, blame the dog." I laughed. "Cheers." We clinked our wine glasses and took a sip. "This is a great pinot. You have perfect taste, as always."

He set down his wine glass. "That I do—perfect taste in wine and women," he said, standing up and reaching out his hand.

"Be careful. Flattery will get you everywhere," I teased.

He took my glass and set it down as well, pulling me up from the chair with very clear intentions. "That's what I was hoping," he said, pulling me close.

Spirit World ❀

$\mathcal{G}$ran's funeral was sad, and I cried a lot, saying another final good-bye. Lou and Sam never left my side, though, and I thought of how grateful I was for that. Losing Gran within six months of losing our parents was certainly a blow. But Lou and I were not alone; Sam and Kristin made sure of that, while our tribe family held us in the palm of its hand.

After the funeral, Lou and I took the ashes of Mom, Dad, and Gran up to the cliff, where the veil between worlds was thin. The tribe and Sam wanted to be there too, but I insisted that it needed to be only me and Lou. We had to walk this road alone, although it comforted me to know they would be waiting for us at the house. We sat on the bench for a while, looking at the urns.

"I don't know how to do this," Lou said with uncertainty in his eyes, reminding me of how he looked when he was little and I helped him learn to tie his shoes or ride a bike. "I don't feel grown-up enough for this. Gran always led on these things."

"We'll say good-bye and release them to the spirit world," I replied, echoing what Gran told me when we'd done this for Grandpa Charles.

"I don't think I can let them go, Kay." Lou held an urn in his hand, and his fingers gripped it tightly. I took a deep breath to gather my strength. I was the big sister and keelalle, and I had to be strong for him. I wished Sam was here.

"We're not letting them go, Lou. We're helping them settle into the spirit world. They are still with us, just on the other side. When Gran came up here, she used to say that her heart was a river, and Grandpa Charles was the sea: even when we couldn't see him, the love still flowed through. Come on. Let's move to the edge," I said.

He nodded, and we stepped toward the fence line at the cliff's edge. I closed my eyes and concentrated on the wind to shift it toward the sea. I lifted up Dad's urn, opened the top, and let the wind lift his ashes and carry them through the veil across the waves.

"Dad, we're naming our son after you, and I promise he'll be a baseball fan too, like you and Grandpa Charles. We'll be OK," said Lou.

It started to rain lightly, more like a mist, and I felt it wash away my tears. "We'll be OK," I said to the wind as it delivered him away.

Lou lifted Mom's urn, opened the top, and held my hand. The wind lifted her away, glimmering in the sky before disappearing into the waves. "Our hearts are rivers, and you both are the ocean," I said, letting the tears continue to fall.

"I miss you every day," Lou whispered.

Letting go of my hand, Lou wiped tears from his eyes and set the empty urn down. He reached over to hug me, and we stood there silently for what seemed a very long time. Eventually, we stepped apart as I reached for Gran's urn. I looked at Lou, and he understood, reaching over to lift the top while I shifted the breeze to release her as well. Her ashes drifted toward the sky and then also disappeared across the waves. "Take care of each other," I whispered.

"Good-bye, Gran," Lou said.

We returned to the bench, sat down, and silently watched the waves. Lou leaned his head on my shoulder, and I put my arm around him. I comforted my little brother, leaning on me as we faced our futures without Mom, Dad, and Gran. "We'll be OK," I whispered. "We'll be OK." After watching the sunset, we knew it was time to go and returned to the car.

Sam met us in the driveway, and I melted into him. "We have a surprise for Lou," he said, looking at the front door. A young, pregnant woman appeared, and Lou rushed up to her.

"You found Ashley?" I asked Sam.

"She called Dorothy's last night, as she hadn't heard from Lou, and he'd given her Dorothy's number. We flew her up here, and I picked her up from the airport this afternoon," Sam explained.

"Thank you. That was very thoughtful. I think he needs her with him now, just like I need you." I hugged Sam tightly.

"So how was it?" he asked.

"Sad…difficult and…sad. But I'm glad it was just the two of us. In a way, it was easier because we didn't have to be *any-thing* for anyone else, like at the funeral with everyone staring."

"Let's go inside. I've made some saffron *arancini,* rigatoni *ai carciofi*, and smoky mac-and-cheese for dinner. The whole tribe council is here too."

I leaned in for a hug. "Thank you," I said. "You are the ocean."

"What does that mean?" Sam asked.

I smiled. "It means that I love you." We held hands and walked into the busy house, full of life, love, and amazing food. In the dining room, nine of us crowded around the farmhouse table, pouring wine and passing dishes as if it were Thanksgiving. Ashley filled the room with joy, and after hearing her bubbly laugh and seeing her face light up each time Lou spoke, I considered her my sister already. I thought of Mom's perfume, and I could smell it—the rose floral she insisted on. Mom was here, and I could feel her joy, seeing all of us together around the table. My attention diverted to the candles around the centerpiece that flickered, almost flashing on and off as if they were controlled by a light switch. No one else seemed to notice. Ashley soon excused herself, leaving to go to sleep early, tired from the trip.

We stayed at the table for another hour, drinking wine and telling stories. My eyes again focused on the flowers in the center of the table between the flickering candles, the snowdrops that Sam had likely handpicked that morning from somewhere nearby. He had brought me snowdrops every week since that first time at the lighthouse. And suddenly I remembered.

"The first flowers of the year, the snowdrops," I whispered to myself. Mom *did* tell me where the journals were hidden, only not in an obvious way. Reflecting for a moment, I took flowers out of the vase and smelled roses. I closed my eyes and could almost feel Mom touch my shoulder. "Thanks, Mom. I miss you," I said quietly as I wiped my sleeve on the corner of my eye.

Sam looked over at me, concerned. "What is it?"

I smiled. "Mom told me where the journals were; I knew this whole time. I just didn't know that I knew. It's the snowdrops!"

He smiled, looking at the flowers. "*That's* why I keep bringing them to you. I didn't really know why, but it must have been Annette somehow..."

I nodded. "Somehow..."

Sam tapped his fork against his wine glass, like a bell. "Everyone, Kay has an announcement to make."

I stood up, and everyone looked at me. "I know where the journals are," I said excitedly.

Klahanee ❄

*A*fter my announcement at the dinner table, we all had a lot to try to explain to Lou.

"Kay, you're saying that you think the story about the copy of the journals is real, that our family has been hiding them for the last two hundred years, and that you think you know where they are?" Louis seemed less excited and confident about this than I did. "Oh, and, that you can change the weather, magically heal people, and see the future."

"I know. It sounds unbelievable," I replied.

"And, John, you're this raven spirit tribe chief who's somehow linked with coyote girl over here, and Sam is her twin soul."

"Yep, you're all caught up now," John said matter-of-factly.

"And you all know that this is some pretty irrational territory, right?" Lou said slowly.

I nodded. "Look, I know this is difficult to believe. I can't explain any of it, but it's real. Come with me. Maybe this will help. Take your coat." I took Lou's hand and walked outside to the backyard.

"I'm going to try and make it snow, just enough to cover the lawn, so you'll believe me. It's important to me that you believe me—you're my tribe."

Lou rolled his eyes. "This is ridiculous, Kay—I mean, coincidence at best with the lightning."

I ignored his protests, closed my eyes, and thought about Sam. I thought about our first kiss. My control had improved, once I'd accepted everything and made the decision to stay home.

"What the…This can't be," Louis said, watching the snow fall only on our lawn while the rest of the sky remained bright blue. His eyes widened like saucers.

I opened my eyes, grabbed Lou's hand, and smiled broadly. "I know, right?"

John added, "You're getting better, Kehlok, more focused. I'm impressed."

"There's got to be *another* explanation," Lou said, reaching out to catch the snowflakes. "But I can't think of one. So all those stories growing up—they were *all*…real?"

"I don't know about that, but seems like a lot of them are," I said.

Sam interrupted. "Are you OK, Lou? You look a little shook up."

"I thought these were tribe secrets, keelalle club members only. Mom wouldn't even tell *dad* anything."

"Sam's in the tribe, now, remember?" John explained. "Sam's native name is Bebe Talapus. Do you know what that means? Tell him, brother," John said, looking expectantly at Sam.

"It means 'Handsome Devil,'" Sam said.

John laughed and then said, "You wish! It means 'man who kisses coyotes.'" Louis laughed hard, beside himself. Sam leaned into me.

"You heard what the chief said. I'm afraid that I'm going to have to kiss you now," he said. I certainly didn't mind.

Louis protested, "Dude! That's my *sister*! I don't need to see that!"

"Blame the *chief*," Sam replied. "I'm merely following orders."

Louis rolled his eyes. I noticed Sam had cut his face shaving and pointed out the cut to Louis. "Lou, do you see this cut?"

"Yes. What about it?" Lou asked.

I kissed Sam on the cheek, exactly over the cut, and it disappeared. Louis's eyes went wide again.

"That's a new one," John said proudly. "I have a cut on my cheek over here. Could you fix that too?" he asked mischievously, primarily to bug Sam.

"No way are you kissing *him*," Sam said adamantly.

I kissed Sam again quickly and said, "Don't worry, babe. That only works for *you*. Sure, John, I'll grab some leaves for that—nature's bandages." Sam looked jubilant, while John laughed.

"OK, so I believe you on this keelalle stuff, and I'm OK with Bebe Talapus over here being in the tribe. Still, Sam, I'm watching you." Lou made a sign with his fingers to indicate he was going to be watching Sam closely.

I walked over and hugged Louis. "Be nice to Sam."

"Can we go back inside now?" Lou asked.

"Oh, yes, of course, let's go back inside," I replied.

"So *where* are the journals then, Kay?" John inquired.

"Well…I'm not *exactly* sure. But I have an idea. I think they're on the land Mom and Dad bought up on Klahanee Street, near Lighthouse Keepers Road by the park—remember that? We have something like two acres up there. Gran and Mom took me there once a year, a special girls-only walk to see the snowdrops. I never thought anything of it, but today, seeing the snowdrops on the table, I just *knew*. I've been asking Gran about this for months, and she always said, 'Ask your mother.' Well, today I think Mom answered me."

"I forgot about that land. I used to go up there in high school and drink beer with my friends," Louis said. "Mom never knew."

"Mom knew *everything* we were up to, often before we did," I said, disagreeing with Lou.

"She didn't know about *that*," Lou argued.

I looked at him sternly, as only an older sister could. "Anyway, the problem is that the journals could be anywhere. There are two acres of land, and those journals are buried somewhere. It could take weeks of digging—months even."

"I'll get the shovels," Sam said. "Let's load up the car."

Louis shook his head. "He does love you, doesn't he?" I grinned like a Cheshire cat. "Still, I've never liked any of Kay's boyfriends before, so don't expect me to like you," he said sternly and protectively.

I intervened. "Lou! Don't be a jerk. I'm going to marry Sam…well…*someday*. Be nice to him."

Louis looked at me in utter astonishment, raising his eyebrows. Sam laughed and put his hand on Lou's shoulder in a friendly pat. "I bet you're more surprised that she said that than that she can control the weather!"

"Damn straight," Lou replied, his mouth wide open.

"It's too late to go out there tonight," I said to Sam. "But we should go tomorrow, Lou. I think we need you there, a whale spirit, to help."

John concurred with the plan. "OK then, we sleep here and, in the morning, investigate the property."

James, Mary, Earl, and Betty, however, had to work the next day and decided they would return to Seaside that night. John bragged about the joys of telecommuting, and Sam said the restaurant could run itself. I knew that neither of them would miss out on a treasure hunt, and I was only too grateful for that, as I knew we needed them.

As I had anticipated, the next morning after breakfast, Ashley volunteered to stay home and make a lunch for us when we returned. I think she also appreciated the extra time alone to rest.

"I never thought I'd say this, but...Bebe Talapus, are you ready to roll?" Lou joked to Sam outside in the driveway, after the guys loaded the shovels in the back of John's truck.

"Get in the car," I said, annoyed, smacking Lou on the back of the head teasingly. My mind flashed to what seemed like a memory of Lou and Sam playing peekaboo with our toddler daughter in the living room and Lou's kindergarten-age son. I stopped for a second, realizing that it was a snapshot of the future, not a memory. Love was the key. I *was* powerful beyond measure—and no longer afraid of anything.

We arrived at the land parcel with only shovels and hope. I remembered that there was a meadow away from the road where the snowdrops appeared every year. Mom and Gran always took me there to see the first flower of the year, and I led the others along, almost on autopilot. I figured the journals had to be in that meadow somewhere. Still a long shot, but at least it limited the search area down from two acres to about half an acre.

The guys followed me along the path, Sam holding my hand like we'd been together for years. It was nice, surrendering to the flow of energy between us. I was all-in now. It took me a while to catch up to him, but the important thing in the end was that I caught up—and that he waited for me.

We could see the snowdrops in the meadow, and suddenly Sam pulled me close to him. "Stop," he urged quietly. "Look!" He pointed to a coyote pacing the snowdrop field. "We should turn back," he said.

"No, it's OK. He won't hurt me. You guys wait here." I walked forward slowly, closer to the coyote, which started growling at the guys behind me. Its teeth and growl should have deterred me, but I continued forward. "It's OK, buddy," I said softly, reaching out my hand. "They're with *me*. I'm Kehlok. Do you remember me? Huh? You know me, don't you?" I said gently, steadily continuing forward.

The coyote stared at me, pacing, and started to howl. Then it stopped pacing across the field and started running directly toward me. I stopped briefly, a little afraid. The coyote stopped as well. I continued ahead, moving slowly. The guys were at least thirty feet behind me, and the coyote was now only five feet ahead of me. It looked at the guys and then back to me while I continued to speak to it soothingly. When I was only three feet away from the coyote, it sat down and then knelt, lowering its head. I reached out to pet it, still talking softly.

"You *do* remember me, or at least you know me," I said, crouching next to it, while petting him on the head. What a rush! This wild animal lay before me like a Labrador retriever. My fear disappeared. "Do *you* know where they are? The journals? Where did Mom hide them?" I asked. I thought to myself that I had to be a little nuts now, talking to a coyote and asking it where the "treasure" was buried. I was instantly reminded of a yoga class I'd gone to once, where they'd eased us into strange poses for over an hour. By the time they'd said, "Put your feet on your elbows while standing on your hands," it'd seemed to be a reasonable thing to do. I laughed a little. "You know where they are, do you, little guy? Kah nesika klatawa? Ikta mike tumtum?" I said in Chinook jargon, asking the coyote where we should go and what it thought.

Suddenly, the coyote sat up and took off running a few steps away, as if it needed the Chinook jargon translation. Then the coyote stopped and turned around to look at me, as if saying, "Come on. Follow me." I followed, and it jumped up like a trained dolphin, happy to perform. We crossed the field to the tree line almost fifty yards away from the guys. I could sense how nervous Sam was, even from here. The coyote smelled the tree trunks as if it were trying to find a place to relieve itself, but then it stopped and started digging. It looked up at me.

"So, you *do* know, don't you? You've been waiting for me. Good boy, my coyote friend. Nika tilikum talapus," I translated again, petting it. The coyote stopped digging. "I'm going to call my friends over now, and you'll probably decide to leave. Thank you for this. Mahsie talapus, mahsie nika tilikum," I continued, translating the last sentence. I bowed my head. The coyote looked up at me and bowed down again. Then it ran away into the dark woods of the forest, howling. I watched it go, and when I couldn't see it anymore, I shouted over to the guys, "Over here! Come on!"

We started digging at the spot marked by the coyote, with Louis and John teasing Sam about kissing that coyote. It didn't bother him or me, though, because every time they mentioned it, Sam would use it as an excuse to kiss me. Louis broke first, eventually begging John to stop mentioning it, so he wouldn't have to see someone kissing his sister. It was a good game all around, as far as I was concerned. Eventually, the hole we were digging got to be at least three feet deep.

"Wait up," Louis said, raising his hand. "I heard something." We dropped the shovels as Louis crawled down in the hole to use his hands to dig. "There's something here, like a metal box," he yelled up. "Hand me the small garden shovel." Soon he pulled up four metal containers, each about the size of four shoe boxes tied together. He lifted them up to John and Sam, who set them aside, and then they helped Louis up.

"The boxes all have combination locks on them," John observed. "Did the coyote tell you the combination for them too?" he joked.

"No, he's not very good with numbers," I responded sarcastically. "What do you think, Lou?"

"Probably your birthday, Kay," Louis guessed.

"Hmm, a birthday, huh? I'm sure it's your birthday then. You are Meriwether Louis Baker, the whale spirit and keeper of knowledge, after all. Mom would have known that you would be here to find the boxes with me. Besides, there's *got* to be a reason she gave you that name."

"When's your birthday, Louis?" John asked. "We'll try that first."

"February twenty-ninth," Louis said.

"A leap year, baby—so how old are you in leap years?" Sam asked.

"I'm twenty-six, Bebe Talapus," Louis replied.

"Ah, but in leap years, you're really only seven! You are a *little* brother, little brother," Sam joked.

Louis looked at him harshly, as if he would say something cutting in response, but then he looked at me and softened. "I suppose so...*bro*. I suppose so."

I beamed at the two of them—the top men in my life accepting each other and getting along. Even though we'd lost Gran only the other day, there was so much joy around this moment. She would have wanted it that way, and somehow

I could feel her delight—and Mom's. I felt it in the air, like a cosmic shower of happiness. Somewhere, even Tamahna and Meriwether Lewis watched over us with joy.

"It worked!" John exclaimed. "The combination is two-two-nine! Come here and look at this!" We hurried over and sat down around the opened box. Inside the metal box sat a plastic box filled with papers that were sealed in a plastic bag and another plastic box full of small items. Elk skin covered the handmade journals with Meriwether Lewis's handwriting in thick, black ink. "There are at least two hundred pages in here, perfectly preserved...and letters," John noted. "And in here there's some red cloth, like from a uniform, some red trading beads, and a silver medal with Thomas Jefferson on one side and an image of a handshake on the other."

"I've read about those medals," Lou said. "Those are the peace medals that Jefferson gave Lewis and Clark to give as gifts to the natives they met on the trail." We all looked at him, surprised at his encyclopedic knowledge. "What? My name *is* Meriwether, and I spend a lot of time at sea with nothing to do but read. Of course I've read a lot about Lewis and Clark," he explained, clearly bristled by our astonishment.

We opened the three other boxes with the same combination and found another three journals of the same size and more letters similarly stored to be protected against the elements. It was incredible. We marveled at the original draft of all of Meriwether's journals from Saint Louis to Fort Clatsop, stored for safekeeping with Tamahna in case his were lost.

"The missing four hundred pages of Meriwether Lewis's journals are in here. And the letters…We've unearthed the greatest love story never told," I said excitedly. "We were erased from history, and now, these will set the record straight."

"What's that in there? This last one has an extra piece of paper, one with blue margins." John handed it over to me.

"It's Mom's handwriting," I said and covered my mouth in surprise. "Sam, will you read it? I won't be able to without… crying."

Sam nodded and read aloud.

> Dear children,
>
> I know that the time will be right to publish these when you find them; science will have advanced to prove our lineage without a doubt. I trust you to get them in the right hands. Mom gave me these boxes when Kehlok was born, for me to be the new caretaker, and I bought this land specifically to hide them here.
>
> I am blessed with the gift of knowing that you will discover them, and I am grateful to have such loving children who care for each other. I love you very much.
>
> And, Louis, I knew about the drinking here, you little rascal.
>
> Love,
>
> Mom
>
> August 1979

"Wow, she wrote that *before* you were born, Lou. She knew your birthday even then," I said, wiping tears from my eyes as I went over to hug Louis.

"Don't make me cry in front of the guys," Louis said.

Both John's and Sam's eyes were already red with tears. "Don't worry, buddy," Sam said. "We're already teary over here." He smiled at me, and I almost forgot to breathe. We all laughed and wiped our eyes. Sam came over and kissed me on the forehead. We each picked up a box and walked toward the car as the coyote howled a farewell.

Papers ❋ March

$\mathscr{I}$t had been a month since we'd discovered the journals, and Lou and Ashley had already returned to start their life together in San Diego. The Smithsonian sent a Lewis and Clark expert from Georgetown University over to review the materials and authenticate them, as I had refused to mail the journals and letters to some nameless bureaucrat. My family spent two hundred years protecting these documents, and if we were going to share them with the world, then I wanted to personally oversee everything.

That meant I now spent my days with Janet Cho as we wore white gloves and poured over the materials. She stayed at the nearby inn, although mostly she spent her days at my house. Fortunately, I liked her. Janet's dedication to accuracy combined with her enthusiasm and knowledge about Meriwether Lewis made me wish I'd paid closer attention in history class.

"More coffee, Janet?" I asked her on Saturday, which was typically a day reserved for me and Sam to spend together. He begrudgingly agreed to hang out with us at my house, because he knew that Janet would be returning to Washington, DC, later that week, and our lives could return to normal soon. Georgetown kindly gave her a month's sabbatical to help the

Smithsonian evaluate the journals, and she had to return to teaching classes and helping to publish these journals as well.

"Yes, please. Oh, this is *another* one of the missing entries from the published journals! I can't wait to rub this into Fitzgerald's face now that the document authentication results came back positive. He's never believed that Lewis wrote daily, despite my thorough thesis research. I *knew* that Major Neely took more than personal items. Eat this, Fitzgerald Harrison! Lewis wrote *every* day!" Janet exulted in her success. Sam started to laugh so hard that coffee almost came out of his nose.

"I'm going to miss you when you leave this week, Janet. I'm so grateful to have found someone we can trust these documents with, who will make certain the full story is told," I said. "I know you'll do it justice."

"Thanks. I'll miss you too, Kay. It's incredible to meet a direct descendent of Meriwether, and that your family managed to preserve these documents across generations is a remarkable gift. Most of us assumed that all the primary source material on the expedition was already out in the world, and then you find this complete treasure trove. I'm going to spend the rest of my career evaluating these materials," she said excitedly. The phone rang, again for the tenth time this morning—mostly media wanting a quote about the journals or academics calling for access to the materials.

Sam glared at me from the other side of the newspaper. "Don't answer it, Kay. It only encourages them," he said.

I smiled and picked up the phone, knowing it wasn't another academic I'd have to disappoint by saying that he or she would have to contact the Smithsonian about accessing the materials after they were catalogued. "August would be perfect," I greeted in place of hello.

"I'm sorry? Is this Kay Baker?" a man asked, sounding confused.

"Yes."

"Hi, Kay. I'm Dr. Jamal Miller at Astoria Medical Center, although you seemed to be expecting my call? Your residency application is very impressive, and I've agreed with Chief Lopez that we'll add you to our intern program here, if you can start in August…Did Chief Lopez already call? How'd you know about August?"

"Oh…um, lucky guess, I suppose."

"Indeed. You know, I'm a little surprised that someone with your qualifications isn't aiming for Portland or Seattle, but we'd be happy to have you join us at AMC."

"Terrific! Oh, thank you so much, Dr. Miller. My mom spoke so highly of you, and I feel very lucky to be accepted in the program."

"Excellent. I'll have the program manager mail you the materials, and we'll see you in August. Call if you have any questions."

"Thank you, Doctor. Thank you!" I hung up the phone and found Sam's gaze. "I got accepted to the Astoria program! No moving!" I announced excitedly.

He jumped up and hugged me close. Both of us were relieved that I could complete my residency just down the road instead of having to move or try a long-distance relationship. Janet stood up and gave me a high five, likewise excited for us, because I had mentioned waiting for the news, and Astoria was the last program I heard back from. Sam beamed and pulled me to him again. We kissed, evidently long enough to make Janet decide she had other things to do. She coughed.

"I should...uh...pack my things and get ready for the flight this week. Kay, is it OK if I pick up the documents on Monday? You guys could use some time off from me, and I have a lot more research to do."

I stepped back from Sam, realizing we had gotten a little carried away. "Oh, sure, that's fine. See you on Monday then."

"Thanks for letting me come by today. I realize it's a Saturday—"

"Sure, of course, no problem. I know you're the right person for this. Thanks for all of your help in getting the documents authenticated and all the work you've done already."

"My pleasure, and congratulations on the residency. I'll see you Monday? Bye, Sam," Janet said, moving quickly to her car.

Sam smiled mischievously. "Finally. I thought she'd never leave. Saturday is *our* day," he said, relieved.

"I know."

His phone rang, and we both cringed. "Only two minutes, I *swear*—it's my brother." I looked disappointed and walked outside to the greenhouse. "Hey, Tony!" he greeted his little brother, who lived in New York.

When I returned ten minutes later, Sam was still on the phone, and he had moved to the kitchen, speaking quietly. I stopped at the screen door, unable to resist eavesdropping.

"Tony, I wish you'd be more supportive...She's *not* a rebound girl...It's not like anything I've felt before, not even

with Rachel. This relationship with Kay is all consuming...
We're *not* moving too fast."

I stepped away from the door as Neb barked. Sam looked
over at me, and I scowled at Neb. "Traitor," I said. Neb wagged
her tail, sat down, and licked my hand in place of an apology.

"Look, let's talk later. I've got to go." He hung up the
phone, and I stepped inside, leaving Neb in the backyard.

"So...How's the fam?" I asked awkwardly.

"My brothers are just...protective," he said, walking over
to me.

"Maybe they're right. Maybe we *are* moving too fast.
Sometimes this scares me, how all consumed I am too, in...
us, like I'll lose myself," I said, reaching up to touch his face.

He leaned in to kiss me. "I found myself the day we met. I
don't make any sense *without* you."

"You always know exactly what to say, and what I meant to
say. Still, what if Tony never likes me?"

"Tony? Don't worry. He'll love you."

"What if he doesn't?" I asked nervously.

"Then I'll beat him up. That's how we boys solve problems," he said with a laugh. "Now, what is it that you know?"

"What are you talking about?" I shrugged and walked into
the kitchen, setting out the herbs I'd cut in the garden. Of
course, he followed like a magnet.

"Oh, I know that look. You *know* something," he persisted.

"Only *part* of something: Janet's going to win a major
award with her next book on Meriwether Lewis," I said. "But
don't say anything to her about it."

He leaned over to me and pushed some stray hair away from my eyes. "You've known this for a while, haven't you?"

"Look, I'm still figuring this out. It's not normal to know the future, and I don't know what I should tell you about it. I mean, what if I tell you something, and then you make a different choice, and that changes everything that was supposed to happen?" I still hadn't told him about seeing our daughter; some things were best kept secret.

"You know that's not what I'm talking about," he said mysteriously.

"What? I don't..." He wasn't making any sense, and he seemed a little nervous.

"How will I ever be able to surprise you when you already know what's going to happen?" he questioned, running his hands through his hair in frustration.

"I don't. It's not like I know *everything*. Often—take right now for example—you are a complete mystery to me, and I have no idea what you're talking about." It was true; sometimes I would see flashes in my mind of the two of us, but so far only twice. There was something about being around him that distracted me.

He looked deep into my eyes for half a minute, searching for something. "OK, then let's get out of here. Let's go to Astoria for the day, just you and me. I think we need a break from this house."

"Astoria? OK, why not? We can celebrate the news of my residency. I'm so glad I don't have to move to Chicago."

"I'm definitely in violent agreement with you on that point."

In the car, he leaned over before putting his seatbelt on. "I'm glad we're staying here too," he said with a kiss.

We had lunch at the bistro under the bridge, enjoying a terrific view of the river and some superb wine from the Yakima Valley. Of course the weather was clear and bright; I figured that occasionally it couldn't hurt to *influence* the weather. After all, I needed to practice, right?

"What time is it?" he asked.

"Time for you to buy a watch," I said, annoyed. "I don't understand why you refuse to get one. This is the second time you've asked me in an hour."

"Watches get in the way. I don't like them. So, what time is it?" he asked again.

I sighed. "It's six o'clock. Maybe we should head back."

"You're probably right. I'll get the check," he said. He paid the bill, and we walked out on the dock toward the parking lot.

"What time is it?" he asked again.

"Seriously? It's like *two* minutes later than the last time you asked. What is going on with you today?" I asked.

"Can't you just tell me what time it is? You know I'll keep asking until you answer," he pestered.

"Ugh! Fine," I replied, exasperated, looking at my watch. "It's five past. Are you happy now?" When I looked up at him, he was kneeling on the ground in front of me, with the sunset over the water behind him. "What are you doing?"

"Our first kiss was right here, on the dock, on February fourteenth at five past six. And now, on March fourteenth, at five past six, I'm asking you, Kehlok Hannah Baker, will you marry me? I'd be lost without you."

I hadn't seen *this* coming. My stunned look made him smile more broadly. "I...Yes! Yes, of course, Samuel Joseph Morandi, I will marry you." He stood up, placed a ring on my finger, and hugged me closely, lifting me up and spinning me around.

"I was so worried all morning that you wouldn't be surprised. But I still have a few tricks up my sleeve to bypass your sly keelalle ways," he whispered into my ear.

"You have your own magic," I whispered.

"*We* have our own magic," he replied.

Unsteady Ground ❀ April

While there were a few people surprised to find us engaged within only six months of meeting each other, those closest to us were not. As John noted, "You're twin souls. Of *course* you're getting married. It would be surprising if you broke up."

I felt a little disappointed that it wasn't bigger news to those around us—even conservative Dorothy didn't bat an eye at the foregone conclusion. I don't know what I expected, but it made me feel Mom's absence. Kristin tried to make a big deal of it after seeing my face fall a little after her initial lackluster response.

Kristin took me wedding-dress shopping and spent at least an hour very seriously discussing the pros and cons of ecru compared to ivory. Ashley also jumped in to help, albeit remotely, seemingly wanting to plan for me the dream wedding that she'd never had after getting married in Vegas. Sam wanted to move in immediately, and I agreed. It was silly to live next door to each other; we were always together. He put his house on the market and soon moved all of his things over to my—*our*—house.

Neither of us wanted a wedding resembling anything that Ashley or Kristin had in mind. We planned a simple November wedding—of course, November 14. I wanted to think of November not as the anniversary of my parents' death but rather as the month I first met Sam. We both wanted to move together toward a future of happiness, replacing the bad memories with the good. Also, by November Lou and Ashley could come up here as their baby would be almost six months old by then.

"What are you measuring now?" I asked Sam, who pointed a measuring tape across the kitchen and into the dining room.

"You said I had *complete* control over the kitchen renovation and that you'd agree with whatever I decided," he reminded me.

"Yes, but we didn't talk about the dining room."

"Kay, the dining room wall cuts off any possibility of expanding the pantry, not to mention a worthwhile fridge or double oven. If we open this up—"

"So the kitchen is going to take up half of the downstairs?" I asked, clearly unconvinced. I put my hand up to my ear. "And what is that noise? It's like radio static or water running. Did you leave the shower running upstairs?"

"What are you talking about? I don't hear anything. Now, look, we take out this wall, and then we have plenty of space for an eat-in kitchen, the island, and of course a pantry."

"Yeah…OK…sure. Whatever you want," I replied distractedly. "I'm going to check upstairs and make sure the shower isn't running or something. You're sure you don't hear anything?"

"I'm sure, Kay. Wait a minute. Hey, are you OK? You look a little freaked out." He moved toward me, placing his hand on my forehead to check my temperature.

"It's probably nothing."

"Hmm…You are a little warm, and you look a little pale. Maybe you should sit down. I'll get you some water," Sam said.

My feet felt unsteady beneath me; something was wrong. My heart started to race. I sat down on the sofa. "Can you bring me the lavender oil too? It's above the fridge." That should help me calm down. Sam soon sat next to me, holding a glass of water and the lavender oil, looking concerned. Suddenly a shot of pain hit my head like lightning, and I cringed at what sounded like thunder inside my brain as I held my hands on my head.

"Talk to me, Kay—what's happening?" Sam asked worriedly.

"Can't you hear that? The thunder…It's like a lightning storm in my brain. It's so *loud*!" I complained in pain.

"Honey, I don't hear anything. Wait, what is that? A howl? Must be Neb in the backyard."

I shuddered. "No, it's a coyote." And suddenly I *knew*. Quickly I stood up and pulled Sam with me to the doorframe of the dining room, and the ground started to shake seconds after we reached it.

"Earthquake!" Sam exclaimed, pulling me close with one hand as his other reached up to steady us on the doorframe. We heard breaking glass as picture frames fall from the wall and vases crash onto the floor while the house shook for close to five minutes. The lights flickered, and then the power went out completely. "Are you OK?" he asked, pulling me closer to him.

"It's Cascadia…the roar before the quake…That's why you couldn't hear it. It's Cascadia—remember?" Once the quake stopped, I instinctively knew that a tsunami was coming—and quickly. I could almost feel the great wave's energy. "Tsunami…We have maybe fifteen minutes before it hits."

"We have to go, Kay! Get in the car. Leave everything!" Sam pulled me down the hallway toward the door, and I stopped.

"No." I could not be moved.

"What are you doing, Kay? We have to leave—*now*!" he urged.

"No, I have to get to the veil at the lighthouse. I can stop this."

Sam stared at me. The realization of what he knew I would do set in. He could see my resolve.

"*You* have to leave," I whispered, barely able to say the words. "Go as far inland as you can and then east to Yakima. Take the motorcycle and don't stop. Don't look back." I tried to blink away a tear so he wouldn't see it. I remembered my dreams of drowning in the sea, and I honestly had no idea if I would be able to stop the wave.

He sat down in the hallway, crushed by my words. I didn't know if I could stop this, and sending him away told him that.

"I won't go without you," he said directly. "I won't." I sat down next to him, and he pulled me close. We froze in time.

"You wanted me to believe in signs and fate, and this is me believing. You have to go, Sam."

We heard the fire sirens blaring in the distance and the neighborhood evacuation in progress, with cars starting and people checking on their neighbors. There was a knock on the door, and we stood still. "Evacuate! Get to the assembly area on Sixty-Seventh! Evacuate!" And the voice moved along to the next house. Car horns honked as people sped toward Sixty-Seventh Street.

Sam touched my face. "Kay, I will *not* leave you, so let's go to the lighthouse."

I shook my head to disagree. "Please," I begged.

"No. You're stronger with me than you are alone. I'm going with you."

We didn't have time to debate this any longer. I reluctantly nodded in agreement, and we went to the car, speeding in the opposite direction of everyone else, toward the powerfully angry ocean. We parked at the now-vacant coast guard parking lot and ran up the hill to the cliff's edge near lighthouse.

We stopped at the fence line, looking down the rocky cliff side on the already violent surf. "Please promise me this is the most insane thing we'll ever do," Sam said loudly over the howling wind and the sound of the crashing waves below.

I nodded. "I hope so, anyway. OK, hold me and don't let go. Whatever happens, don't let go." He pulled me in close for a kiss, possibly our last; it was more powerful than the storm.

"What do we do?" he asked.

I tried to remember the song. What had Saghalie done? My mind raced. *Saghalie held fast like a mountain…She turned the power of the sea…Cascadia bowed and turned…Diving deep back in the sea…* I took a deep breath. Saghalie had turned the ocean against itself—that's what I needed to do. I could feel Sam's fear and anxiety, and I knew that for this to work, he had to channel his love, not his fear. I kissed him again. "Close your eyes and think of our first kiss…and think of…our daughter," I said over the wind.

He nodded, and his eyes teared up. "We're going to have a little girl?" I could feel his fear fade into love and joy.

"This power is derived from love. Don't give in to fear. Remember, we have our own magic." My eyes softened as I wiped a tear away and then turned to face the ocean while Sam held tight. The tsunami's roar was deafening, as we both now heard it rolling toward us. The great wave stood tall in the horizon, now maybe only five minutes away from ground fall. Even from the high cliff, it seemed to tower above the surf like a skyscraper. I closed my eyes to focus on finding a way to sync into the power of the energy pushing toward us. Rain pelted us, and I ignored it; all my energy focused on the wave.

I imagined the whale spirit pulling the tsunami energy deep into the darkest depths of the ocean. I felt powerful and opened my eyes to see the great wave in the distance. The wave slowed, but did not stop. I had to find the strength to push back harder.

Over the wind I heard John's voice clearly; he was singing. It was the coyote-raven hotline, which evidently only seemed to work in emergencies. I heard his voice over drums and the other tribe members' voices belting out a song over the wind and rain. "*Kehlok* turned the power of the sea, so strong she would not break…Come on, everyone, louder! *Make* her hear us! Come on, coyote girl, hear us and tap into this!" And I instantly understood that the tribe was there; everyone was lined up on the beach at John's house in Seaside, watching the wave on the horizon.

None of them evacuated, because they believed in me. They ran toward the danger, all of them. And I didn't need to *see* them to know they were there; I felt it. As a tribe, we were unstoppable; this wave would not crush us. I had to protect the tribe, Sam, and everyone on the Western Seaboard. This was my destiny.

"Kay, it's working! It's slowing down! Come on. Let's send it back where it came from," Sam said. "You've got this." He kissed my cheek.

Instantly everything clicked, as if I suddenly knew how to fly a fighter jet after years of hearing stories about them. I separated my emotions and tapped into the energy of Sam and the tribe. The wave stopped and stood still, balancing my resistance.

I lifted my arm to push the winds and turn the great wave back, deep into the sea. Sam raised his arm along with mine, steady as granite. Like the rock cliff we stood upon, we held fast. The wall of water dropped by a third, bowing in partial retreat. It wasn't over yet, though. I realized that the wave was still strong enough to make landfall. My resistance needed to broaden across both the Oregon and Washington coasts.

Extending my reach required tapping into more power. I called out loudly into the wind.

"Tyee Kaka Kloshe Nanitch, I hear you. Raven Guard, call the keelalles! All of them. This isn't over yet."

"I don't know all of their names," I understood John over the wind.

"I do, just repeat after me. I don't have enough power to stop the wave without them."

"Are you talking to…John?" Sam asked. "How can I help?"

"Yes, just repeat everything I say. I need the power of the veil, from the spirit world," I explained for the benefit of both John and Sam. I pulled in the power of the veil, calling out to the spirit world for generations of keelalles to stand beside me. "Raven Guard and Kehlok call upon the ancestors to hear our tribe and help us from the spirit world: Saghalie, Kehlokkimta, Tanha, Sahhali, Tamahna, and Kehlok, Annie…Hannah and…Annette: stand with us now at the veil."

I repeated the names again, pausing after each name to hear it echoed by John and Sam. My arms were extended directly ahead of me, and I pushed them out widely, spreading my arms almost like broad wings protecting Sam and the seaboard behind me. Pushing back with a powerful force, I felt the energy surge away from us. The wind shifted, pulling the tide out forcefully, and the great wave disappeared deep into the ocean. After a standstill of almost five minutes, we prevailed. Almost as quickly as the wave threatened the coast, it disappeared into the ocean depths, returning a calm, peaceful sea.

Instantly the rain stopped and the clouds cleared as gentle waves lapped the beach like a dog drinking from its bowl.
I closed my eyes to catch my breath and fell to the ground,
exhausted.

In Between ❀

I looked around for Sam, noticing that an eerie silence had settled in. The waves shifted mutely, and the trees swayed silently from an imperceptible wind. My heart beating in my ears was the only sound. I looked around me, and the lighthouse was gone; only the land and the ocean remained. Anything manmade had vanished. I blinked rapidly to refocus, because this couldn't be happening. I panicked.

"Sam! *Sam*? Where are you?" I screamed, my voice echoing as the only sound.

Desperate to find him, I called out again. I could smell his cologne in the air, but I couldn't see him. My heart raced, and I screamed out for him again, frightened. I heard footsteps swishing through the grass, gentle and deliberate, the only sound outside of my beating heart. I turned.

"Mom!" I ran to her and hugged her closely; she was real and warm. "I can't believe it! You're here, and it's really you." And then I realized that it wasn't Sam who had gone; it was me. "I'm…I'm…If you're here, and he's…then I'm…*dead*?" I could barely say the word. Mom put her hand on my shoulder, and then somehow instantly Dad appeared next to her, holding her hand.

"Kehlok, you're *in between*: not home or in the spirit world. We are in the veil, meeting you between worlds," Mom explained as Dad leaned in to hug me.

"But how did I get here? How do I get back to Sam?" I asked, panicked.

"Time passes differently in the in-between, Kay. Here you are both out of time and out of place," Dad said. "You can't go back until your body recovers, and you can't move into the spirit world until your body dies."

Suddenly Gran appeared with Grandpa Charles and Uncle Steve. They all looked healthy and felt as real to me as Sam had only moments ago. "I stopped it...Cascadia. It's safe again for hundreds of years."

"Yes, that was always your destiny, child," Gran said. "We helped where we could, giving you strength—all of us." She pointed toward the keelalles who'd instantly appeared alongside my family. I knew each of them without introduction. Saghalie embraced me, the most powerful of our line before me and the first to hold Cascadia back. I felt her pride, and she looked at me knowingly like a veteran meeting another. She smiled, and we bowed toward each other.

"You did—all of you, you helped. Thank you," I said. "I couldn't have done it without your help."

Saghalie reached for my hand. The movements of her mouth were out of sync with her words, as if she were in a movie that had been dubbed in English. "You are far more powerful than me, Kehlok. I couldn't keep the great wave from making landfall. Although I protected thousands of people in several tribes, many died that day in areas where the wave reached the land.

I think your twin soul and the Raven Guard made all the difference; they amplified your power. I sent my twin soul away to keep him safe." Her eyes shone with pride and amazement. I felt humbled and honored.

"I tried to send Sam away," I said. "With all the keelalles, Sam, and Raven Guard, I had the power of both worlds. I will name my daughter after you, Saghalie," I said, honestly believing it was the highest honor I could award her. She smiled so widely I could see every tooth. I returned the smile and we hugged.

"Our tribe has guarded this coast for hundreds of years," Mom explained. "Saghalie held back the Cascadia tsunami in 1700 after the eight-point-seven quake, saving many lives despite part of the wave still making landfall in other areas. That is why we keelalles have always lived near the veil."

Gran added, "Kehlok, you stopped the entire tsunami after a *nine*-point-three quake. None of us even knew that was possible."

Mom continued, "You were destined to protect the people, and even in the modern world, you can still do so much more...maybe cure cancer? None of us knows your full destiny, but there is more for you to do, I hope."

I looked at the keelalles and my immediate family. "How long can you be here?" I asked.

"We can stay as long as you are in the in-between. If your body loses the fight, we will take you to the spirit world," Dad said gently.

Tamahna rushed toward me, looking desperate. Her words similarly seemed dubbed, like a universal translator worked in the veil across languages. "Please," she begged. "Please help my Meriwether to find me in the spirit world. His ashes must be sent through the veil by the wind to help his spirit find me. There are many spirit worlds, and he is lost. I can't leave this world because I might never find my way back and lose him forever. Look in the third journal binding, where you will find a letter hidden that will tell you everything you need to know. Please, help him find me. Promise me. Please?"

Her distress pulled at my heart. I thought about how I would feel to be separated from Sam in any world, spirit or otherwise, and felt her pain. "Yes, I will try. I promise," I said. She hugged me tightly with tears of joy. Then she stepped back, having said her peace, allowing Gran to step forward again.

"You have brought our family such joy, Kay," Gran said proudly. "It is a miracle that we can meet here—and very rare, from what we understand. Especially to stay here so *long*—most people are only here for a few seconds or less."

"I have so many questions…Wait! What's happening?"

Their distinct features started to fade, like overly air-brushed photos. I realized that our time was limited and reached for Mom and Dad. "We miss you so much. Lou's going to have a baby boy, and he's married now to Ashley, who is wonderful. He's so happy. I'm so happy with Sam, and we're getting married," I blurted quickly, unsure of how much time we had.

"We know all of this, Kay. Sometimes we come by and visit, but you know that," Mom said, as her features blurred further and a thick fog crept over everything in the landscape.

I then felt Sam holding my hand tightly, anchoring me to the world and pulling me from the in-between. I looked at my hand, and when I looked up for Mom and Dad, they had vanished, as suddenly as they had appeared. I closed my eyes.

Waking Up ✤ May

When I opened my eyes, I instantly felt pain and exhaustion. Looking up, I realized I was in a hospital bed with Sam holding my hand. Upon noticing my slightest movement, Sam stood up with a start.

"She's awake! She's *awake*!" he announced excitedly. "Kay, are you OK? Are you in pain? Stay with me, Kay—*don't* fall asleep, whatever you do. Someone hurry...She's awake!"

My eyes were heavy, and I felt as if I had been awake for years. Sam touched my face urgently. "You didn't let go," I whispered.

"Never. Kay, stay awake!" he urged.

Doctors and nurses flooded the room, pushing ahead of Sam and asking him to step aside. His concerned look amplified when he had to let go of my hand.

"Kay...Kay...I'm Dr. Williams. Do you know where you are?"

A nurse started adjusting the bed so that I would sit up.

"I'm really tired," I mumbled.

"I know that, Kay, but we need you to stay awake, OK? Now, do you know where you are?"

"Hospital?" I asked.

"Yes, that's right. You're at Astoria Medical Center," he said, checking my eyes while a nurse took my blood pressure. "Do you know what month it is?"

"April...Sam? Where's Sam?" I asked, frightened by all the activity in the room. I felt shattered.

"I'm right here," Sam said, moving in close to be able to put his hand on my shoulder, making me feel stronger.

Leon flew into the room, obviously having run from somewhere else in the hospital. "How is she?" Leon asked.

"She's responsive and blood pressure is returning to normal, although she's groggy and disoriented. We've administered a stimulant to keep her awake for a while longer," Dr. Williams explained.

"Leon? What's happening?" I asked.

"You gave us quite a scare, Kay. You've been in a coma for twenty-five days now."

"Twenty-five *days*...coma?" I felt that I had only been out for minutes in the in-between; the time in the veil was still vivid in my mind.

Sam gripped my shoulder as my body started to wake from the stimulant. "Sam brought you in the night of the tsunami warning—you fell down when trying to reach the evacuation assembly point," Leon explained.

"Yes," I concurred. It was a good story, considering that they would commit me to a psych ward if I said that we'd stopped the tsunami with magic. "Diagnosis?" I asked, words still catching up with my brain processing, like a slow reboot.

"Kay, you presented with symptoms similar to being struck by lightning, although there were no burns. We're not entirely sure what happened to you, actually. It's like your body had a massive electrical surge but not a heart attack," Leon explained.

Sam kissed my head and smoothed the strays away from my eyes. They tested everything—reflexes, memory, vision—and then, after I ate something, allowed me to go back to sleep, although with strict instructions to wake me every four hours. Sam stayed with me, sleeping on the small sofa in the room.

The next day I felt stronger, and I was even able to walk around the ward a bit with a lot of help from Sam. On our walk I learned what had happened while I was *out*.

"I've never been so scared in my life," Sam said when we were finally alone without medical staff or visitors hovering. "After the wave disappeared in the ocean, you fell lifelessly to the ground. I thought you were dead, but then I could feel your pulse, so I carried you to the car and broke every speed limit between the lighthouse and the hospital. You've been here ever since."

"It must have been terrible for you, Sam. I'm so sorry."

He smiled. "That's my Kay," he whispered gently. "Only *you* would apologize about saving the Western Seaboard and then falling into a coma."

"We did it, though, didn't we?"

"Yes. It's been all over the news, and several scientists have been in town, all trying to figure out why the nine-point-three Cascadia earthquake didn't destroy the coast with a tsunami, or how a six-hundred-meter wall of water just disappeared into the ocean. There were power outages and places damaged by the major earthquake, but the waves didn't get any higher than they do at high tide. Although no one can explain how a tsunami 'disappeared' into the ocean, everyone agrees that, had it made landfall, it would have been devastating," Sam explained.

"We need to keep it a secret," I said.

"Don't worry. No one would believe it anyway," he said with a laugh. "There is a guy in town asking a lot of questions, though, and he's also been bugging John. Some sort of geophysics professor. He's been asking everyone about the tribal legend of a medicine woman stopping the 1700 Cascadia tsunami. He seems to think that perhaps there's a reason the scientists can't explain what's happened."

"Hmm…Like you said, no one else will believe it. Imagine what would happen if people knew the truth—the world isn't ready for that. Besides, we'd never have a chance at a normal life if people knew."

When we returned to the room, John sat in the chair, waiting. "There she is," he said warmly, standing up to hug me while Sam stood by to help me back into the bed. "It's good to see you awake again, Kehlok."

"It's good to be back in this *world* again. Thank you for mobilizing the tribe on the beach. I heard you."

John smiled, and Sam patted him on the back, having evidently already heard the story from John at some point. "Glad we could help. Amazing power, Kehlok," he gushed. I nodded in agreement. "Thanks for saving my beachfront property," he added and laughed to lighten the conversation.

"Kay, I was telling John our plans about a beach wedding, and he offered up his place. Isn't that great?" Sam asked.

"Wow, that's…wow," I said, trying to hide my disapproval.

"So, we're in then," Sam said. "Thanks, brother."

"My pleasure! It's the least I can do for the keelalle who saved the West Coast from destruction. What happened to you anyway?"

"I think my body needed time to recover. It took a lot of energy," I explained, trying to skip talking about the wedding venue change. "And...this might sound a little crazy. Could you close the door?"

Sam pulled the door closed. "I think both of us can handle crazy by now," he said.

"Well, after the wave retreated into the sea, I somehow went *into* the veil, in between the spirit world and our world. But I was still here, yet not fully here."

"Like some sort of out-of-body experience?" Sam asked.

"Yes. Are you sure that you *still* want to marry me?" I replied anxiously.

He leaned in close. "I've never been so sure of anything in my entire life," he said with a smile, kissing my forehead. I blushed.

"Good," I caught my breath. "So, in the veil, I saw my parents and Gran...and all the keelalles. I felt like I was there with them for only minutes. Anyway, it was incredible."

"How did you come back?" John asked.

"Sam—he somehow pulled me back. I felt him holding my hand, and when I looked to see him, I woke up here. I can't believe I was out for twenty-five days, because it felt like five minutes."

Sam reached for my hand and was about to say something when he was interrupted by a knock on the door. Kristin appeared with a vase full of irises. "How's the patient?" she asked, setting the flowers on the side table before coming over to give me a hug.

"I'm great, thank you. The irises are beautiful—my favorites."

She hugged me tightly. "Leon's home with Grady so I could come over. He said you looked really well, and you do."

"Do you know John? He's from the tribe," I said as an introduction.

"Yes, we've met. You forget that we've been visiting you in rounds for weeks now. All except for this one here," she said, tugging at Sam's shoulder. "He *refused* to leave you, and he wouldn't let go of your hand. I only managed to get him to change clothes and shower if John *and* I were here with you. Neb stayed with us, and now of course Grady wants a dog, so thanks for that. John and I read a lot of books together. Did you hear any of them? Leon says that sometimes patients can hear those in the room."

"I'm sure it all helped," I said, feeling moved by the news that Sam wouldn't leave my side. He hadn't told me that part.

Sam blushed at my gaze. "I didn't want you to wake up alone," he said simply. My heart swelled.

John added, "She's fine with the wedding at my house, so you can keep planning for a beach wedding."

Kristin looked at me confused. "A beach wedding in *November*, Kay? The weather will be *terrible*. You *can't* be serious."

Sam and John smiled. "I'm sure that Kay and Sam will bring their own weather," John said.

"Well, I'm certainly not going to argue with the bride. We'll order some outdoor heaters and tents to make it work. Have you talked to Lou yet? He's called every day, and he's been sick with worry."

"Yes, yesterday. Sam made sure of it," I said. "The baby will be born today. I'm sorry to have to miss it."

"Did they schedule a C-section then?" Kristin asked.

"No, it's just...my *guess* anyway, based on what...um...you know," I stammered.

"I'm going to ignore that, medicine woman," Kristin said with a flick of her hand. "I'm alive and cancer-free today because of you, so I'm not going to ask questions about things I don't understand." She grinned. "Don't you boys need to get a coffee or something so we girls can chat?"

Sam looked uncomfortable about leaving me. John pulled his arm. "Come on. Let's let these girls talk about *you*," he said. Sam stopped at the doorframe and looked at me.

"I'll be fine," I told him. "Can you bring me back an Americano? The coffee here is terrible, and I think I've slept enough for one month." He nodded and made sure that Kristin would stay with me until they returned.

"Boy, that fiancé of yours is something else. I think if he had to choose between being with you and breathing, he would choose you."

I blushed. "I think I would choose him over breathing too," I said. "So, you approve then?" I asked.

"Of course! After all, it was *my* idea in the first place, if you remember."

It felt good to laugh. "Yes, I remember very well. So, I was thinking that the ecru dress from that Portland shop is the one. Remember? The strapless mermaid gown with the tulle?"

"That was my favorite too!" Kristin clapped. "I'll call them to reserve it, and we'll go to Portland for the fitting once you can leave this joint. Leon said maybe this week?"

"Yes, they think that as long as I continue to improve, I should be home by Thursday," I confirmed.

"I'm so glad that Sam's living with you now. I can't imagine you being home by yourself after this. His house sold two weeks ago to a professor who'll be working at Grays Harbor College."

"Yeah, he told me. I'm surprised it sold so quickly. Cape Disappointment is hardly a hot real-estate market."

"It's meant to be, I suppose. Your new kitchen is gorgeous, by the way."

"What? How can it be done already? We had only talked about it before—"

I again had forgotten how long I'd been out.

"He wouldn't leave the hospital, so Sam had me and Dorothy supervising and reporting back when we had time. Sam wanted to make sure it was all done before you got home. He wanted to surprise you, and I think he needed to hold onto something. Making all those calls to the contractor while he was watching you sleep gave him something to cling to."

"So you're telling me that I need to love that kitchen, even if I don't?"

She grinned. "Oh, you will love it. It's beautiful! You might not be able to make coffee or cook an egg using the high-tech chef's appliances that he bought, but it is a gorgeous kitchen." We were laughing when the guys returned with coffee.

"Americano, my lady," Sam said with a smile.

"Thank you."

"Kay, did they tell you about the rumor in town?" Kristin asked.

"No. What rumor?" I asked.

"Scott's probably at fault. He can't help himself in terms of causing trouble, or he wants Amy to like you—either way it's a lost cause. Anyway, people are saying that you stopped the tsunami with your *Indian princess* superpowers. Outlandish, right? Imagine, stopping a tsunami...Like that's possible! I don't care what those scientists say. There's an explanation. These small towns delight in silly gossip, I know, but please...such an outrageous thing for people to say, *even* about you," Kristin said.

Sam, John, and I sat silent for a minute, unsure of how to react. Finally, I forced a guffaw. "Absolutely ridiculous! I've been in the hospital the whole time."

"That's what I keep telling people. You should move to Astoria and leave Ilwaco and Cape Disappointment," she said for the twelfth time since I had moved back home.

"But it's my home," I replied.

Sam faked a cough. "*Our* home," he corrected.

Dr. Williams came in. "I see everybody's in to visit today. Hello, Sam," he added, evidently having seen him here the whole time. "I have good news. We all agree that you can go home tomorrow, as long as you continue to progress as you have been and there are no problems overnight."

"I can't wait to get home. Thank you, Doctor," I said.

Sam exhaled fully, as if I'd received a stay of execution. Kristin and John likewise let out a sigh of relief. "So you'll be home on the twenty-seventh then. That's great," Sam finally said with tears in his eyes. He looked away from me briefly. He was hiding something from me, and I looked concerned, although my thoughts were soon interrupted.

"Lou..." I said. Sam's phone rang. "It's Lou! The baby news!" I announced excitedly, reaching for the phone. Sam nodded that I was right and handed it over without answering it. "Congratulations, Lou! How is baby Henry Meriwether Baker?"

"How'd you...I didn't tell you the full name—but then again you also knew he'd be born in May and not in June," Lou replied.

I laughed. "Keelalle ways, remember? It's a good name."

"I wish Mom and Dad were here to see him. He's so beautiful," Lou boasted.

"I know for a fact that Mom and Dad are there. You just can't see them," I replied. "Hey, good news! Doc says I can go home tomorrow, as long as everything continues to be fine overnight."

I heard Lou gulp. "Tomorrow? That's great! So you'll be home on the twenty-seventh." He took a breath, and I could hear the baby cry. "I've got to get back to Ashley. She's doing great, by the way, and she'll be delighted to hear you'll be home tomorrow. I wanted to call and let you know...I wanted to talk to you. I love you, sis."

"I love you too. Go on and take care of your family. We'll visit you soon."

Lou was hiding something from me too. Both Lou and Sam knew something that they weren't telling me. I smiled through my concern.

Home Again ❀

As expected, I was released from the hospital the next evening, and Sam took me home. I struggled to believe that it had been a month since I'd last seen the house, and I was excited to see the new kitchen. Sam opened the door dramatically, still holding me as if I were a fragile china doll. Even Neb didn't jump up as usual; she waited by the door, wagging her tail and licking my hand.

"Neb, sit," Sam ordered. "Well? What do you think?" he asked expectantly.

I surveyed the new kitchen and dining room, noticing how it looked like something in a magazine. The shiny white cabinets, the white marble countertops and island, and the white subway tile along the walls screamed perfection. Sam had found a faultless shade of mustard for the paint that we'd discussed. "It's beautiful," I said, still marveling at the fact that we had only just talked about it *yesterday*, to me at least, yet here we were in our new kitchen.

Sam grinned. "This is Barry," he said, pointing to a complicated espresso machine that took up an entire corner.

"Barry? You've named the appliances?"

"Barry the barista! What? People name their cars, and I name appliances. He's Italian, so his real name is Bernardo, but he prefers Barry."

I nodded and leaned in to kiss Sam's cheek, charmed by his eccentricity. "Barry's kind of intimidating," I said. "Like I'll first need to learn rocket science or neurosurgery before being qualified to make a cup of coffee."

"Don't worry. He only *looks* intimidating. Underneath this complex exterior lies the heart of a simple Tuscan boy whose *only* dream is to make the best coffee in the world," Sam said.

I laughed. "And the stove?" I asked.

"Mama Maria, the mother of the kitchen."

"She's a big mama. When will we need *eight* burners?" I asked.

Sam put his hands up. "I'm a chef! When *won't* we need eight burners?" He raised his eyebrows and then smiled. "And this is the dishwasher, Ned, which is short for *netto*. It means 'clean' in Italian."

"Wow, you've spent some time thinking about these names." His excitement about the kitchen and having me home to see it was palpable. He squeezed my hand. "Maybe I can meet the rest of the kitchen tomorrow. For now, I think I'd like to take a shower and get to sleep. It's been a long day." He agreed.

"I'm glad you're home, Kay," he whispered, pulling me close.

"Me too…me too," I said.

I woke up early, before the sun, at around four thirty. Unable to fall back asleep, I watched Sam sleep for a while; then I decided to go downstairs and make some coffee. Downstairs I found Barry waiting for me, and I soon located the user manual, although it might as well have been written in ancient Aramaic. I removed the portafilter, took out the steam wand, pulled out the portafilter basket, and then gave up. Neb sat at my feet, staring up at me. I decided to take her for a walk and find some coffee downtown. The best part of living in a fishing village was that there was always a coffee shop open really early in the morning, for the fishermen.

"Come on, Neb," I whispered. "Let's get some coffee." I looked at the espresso machine and narrowed my eyes, annoyed. We headed downtown, with Neb stopping every ten feet to sniff something or mark her territory, of course. Soon enough, we were at the harbor, and I found that the small shed coffee shop on the docks was indeed open, as I had hoped. Some fishermen had already pulled out for the day, and others were still readying their boats.

"Good morning, Sheila."

Sheila Wilkes was Scott's mom. Scott had started a few of these small shed coffee shops throughout the area, which turned out to be a lucrative business. His mom helped out on the early-morning shifts at the dock, as her husband was a fisherman and she was up anyway.

"Bless my stars, if it isn't Kay Baker! Dear, it's good to see you doing so well and out of the hospital. We were all pulling for you. Well, I'd be lying if I said that included Amy, but you know what she's like. She's equal opportunity—doesn't like *anybody.*" Sheila winked kindly, acknowledging her known dislike of her daughter-in-law. "I was always hoping you'd marry Scottie, but it wasn't meant to be, I suppose."

"Not meant to be," I responded lightly. "And how's Stan?"

"Oh, thanks for asking! He's out on the water already this morning, but his arthritis is acting up again. You don't happen to have any of that ginger cayenne salve your mom made, do you? It's the only thing that ever helped him."

"I can make you some today, and we'll drop it by the house tonight," I told her.

"Bless you, dear. Your mom would be so proud of you, God rest her. Lots of us around these parts know it was *you* that kept the wave away, Kay. I know you'll never admit it, but I'd like to thank you just the same. We would have lost everything if it had made landfall. My Stan said that he heard from Willis Jackson, who heard from Billy Cooper, that Jerry Reynolds was out on his boat that night, and he saw that terrible, skyscraper of a wave on the horizon as he sped inland to escape it. Anyway, Jerry told Billy that the wave was moving fast and then it slowed, stopping for about five minutes until it broke by a third. In minutes after that, the big wave simply vanished into the ocean. Billy told Willis who told Stan that Jerry also saw a woman up on the cliff with her arms spread out wide open, as if she was holding her ground against the wave. Stan told Willis that he thinks it was you. Willis agreed."

I didn't know what to say. My family's history was always a gossip point for this town, and had we lived in Salem, Massachusetts, back in the day, the keelalles certainly would have been victims of the trials. We were often the outsiders,

Julie Manthey

even though people started relying more and more on Mom and Gran for help. It felt strange to be recognized so openly by the community for our keelalle ways.

"Well...Sheila," I demurred.

"Oh, I've gone and stepped in it! I don't want to make you nervous, girl, but know that we're thankful. Coffee is on us. What will you have?"

"A large Americano, please. Are you sure? I'm happy to pay," I said.

"Your money is no good here, sugar. How's Sam holding up? He must be happy to have you home again. No one has seen him in town for weeks, and that new chef he hired isn't nearly as good."

"Sam's doing well, thanks. It's been tough on him."

"It's all behind you now. Here's to a fresh start. Can I get you anything else? A scone maybe? A cookie?"

"No thanks, this is perfect. Thanks very much, and we'll come by later with the salve for Stan."

"Bless you, dear," Sheila said gratefully.

Neb and I watched the sun rise above the water before returning home. Sam was still asleep when we came in, so I opened my laptop and decided to catch up on what I had missed over the last month. I read about the earthquake, the theories on why it hadn't devastated the coast, and how they were explaining the resulting tsunami wave that returned to the sea. I read the latest on the Middle East and learned that my favorite TV show had been canceled. I had missed a lot in a month. The hardwood floor squeaked upstairs, and I knew that meant Sam was awake. He called out for me in a panic.

"Kay? Kay! Kay! Where are you?" he hollered out, nearly stumbling down the stairs in a rush.

"I'm here! It's OK. I'm here." I walked over to hug him and saw his face was whiter than the kitchen cabinets. He pulled me close and held tight.

"I woke up, and you weren't there, and I realized it was the twenty-eighth, and I thought that…" he said quickly, words spilling out.

"Hey, it's OK. I'm here," I consoled him. "Come on. Let's sit down and you can tell me about it—whatever it is that you and Lou have been hiding."

We sat down on the sofa, and he kept his hand on my knee as if making sure I wouldn't float away. "I promised Lou I wouldn't say anything," he said.

"I don't care what you promised Lou. Something's wrong, and I need you to talk to me."

He looked over at me. "Where'd you get the coffee?" he asked, noticing the paper coffee cup on the table.

"No changing the subject, Sam. Tell me." I glared at him, refusing to break my gaze.

"Today's the twenty-eighth," he said, touching my face as if to confirm I was there.

"Yes, and what's so special about the twenty-eighth? Lou was cagey on the phone yesterday too."

"As you know, coma patients who don't wake up after thirty days tend not to *ever* wake up. Because we're not married yet, the doctors only spoke to Lou, which is why I called him every day. Lou had to make a decision, and he…and I…

agreed that if you didn't wake up by…we'd let you go on the twenty-eighth."

I took a deep breath as my mind struggled to comprehend what Sam had said. For weeks now, he and Lou had been dealing with the possibility that today would be the day they unplugged me from the machines and let me go. I could only imagine the painful burden they carried. No wonder Sam had been so clingy; this had shaken him.

"That would have been the right thing to do. So when you woke up and I wasn't there——" I said quietly.

"I thought maybe yesterday was a dream and that…"

I leaned in to hold him close. "I'm so sorry. I can't imagine what you've been going through. It's OK. I'm OK," I said. We sat together quietly for a long time.

"I should take Neb out for a walk. Will you come?" he asked.

"I took her out around five and got some coffee downtown. Saw Sheila at the coffee shed on the docks—and, oh, that reminds me: today I need to make up a salve for Stan. His arthritis is flaring up again."

"Sheila and Stan are good people," Sam said. "Too bad about Amy." He rolled his eyes.

"Sheila wouldn't let me pay for the coffee. She told me about the town gossip related to the wave. Kristin wasn't kidding."

"The Jerry Reynolds story? Well, it's a small town, and people talk."

"I know, and I think it's harmless. Nobody will believe them anyway. Maybe it's in our favor. The truth is stranger than fiction."

Sam yawned and stretched like a bear waking up from hibernation. "I haven't slept that well in a month. It's nice to be home and sleep in our own bed again. That hospital sofa was like sleeping in the backseat of a car. I could use some coffee. Want another one? How about Barry and I whip up some Americanos?" he proposed, pulling my hand to lead me into the kitchen.

"Um...about Barry..." I said unsteadily.

Sam soon saw the chaos I had left behind, with the portafilters, baskets, user guide, and other random parts dotting the countertop. "Oh no, Barry! She disassembled you!" He turned to me. "What did Barry ever do to you?" he asked.

"Oh, Barry *knows*. He had it coming," I teased.

Sam laughed loudly, and it made me happy to see him so blissful again. "And you certainly showed him. Don't worry, Barry. You'll be right as rain in no time. Chef Morandi is here to save the day. Two Americanos coming up."

I thought again about the significance of today as I opened the new pantry to find the lavender oil. Sam had thoughtfully set up a whole side of the pantry for the homemade medicine stores that were previously stashed all over the kitchen. Dabbing some lavender oil on my wrists, I brought some in for Sam as well. He could use something to help keep him calm throughout the day. Pulling his hand away from the espresso machine, he looked up at me.

"What's this? Smells girly," he protested slightly, as I held his hand and rubbed some of the oil on his wrists and on his neck.

"Something to help you relax today," I said. "Keelalle trick," I explained as I could feel the muscles in his neck start to loosen.

"I almost lost you," he whispered.

"The key word is *almost*. You didn't lose me. I'm right here."

"I know what else would help me relax," he said roguishly.

"You don't know how to get Barry to work either, do you? You're stalling," I replied.

He groaned and rolled up his sleeves to fix Barry while I slipped out to the garden for cayenne, ginger, turmeric, and some mint. It wasn't the same as Mom's salve recipe, but I knew it would be stronger, and the mint would make it smell better. After succeeding with Barry, we drank our coffees in the kitchen and read the paper while the salve mix steeped on the stove.

Lost and Found ❖

Sam handed me a page from the newspaper, pointing to a book review. The novel was about someone who traveled the world in a sailboat.

"That could be us, Kay. We should buy a boat and, for our honeymoon, cruise around the world on it for like a year," he said.

"What? Who has a *year* to take a vacation like that?" I asked, unconvinced. "What happened to the week in Tuscany? I liked that idea," I said. Suddenly I remembered. The book… Tamahna. How could I forget? I stopped short. "I have to call Janet," I said quickly, reaching for my phone.

Sam looked at me curiously. "No, we're not taking Janet to Tuscany with us. I'm putting my foot down," he joked.

"Aha! I *knew* you remembered. Tuscany is a *honeymoon*. A year on a small boat in the middle of the ocean is a cautionary tale. Hush now, I need to talk to Janet. I remembered something important," I said.

"But it's six in the morning. She's asleep," he grumbled.

"It's nine in DC, so she's at work. Shush! It's ringing."

Janet answered quickly. "Hey, Kay, how are you? I've been trying to reach you for *weeks*. What happened?"

"Oh…right. Sam didn't tell you?" I asked, glaring accusingly at him. He shrugged.

"Tell me what? No, obviously. Anyway, I was talking to Fitzgerald Harrison two weeks ago, and do you know what he said?"

I stopped her abruptly. "It'll have to wait. This is important."

"You've changed your mind about releasing the journals, haven't you?" she asked nervously.

"No, not that. Are you with them now?"

"Yes, of course, they are on my desk as we speak," she confirmed.

"OK, the third one—check the binding. I think there's something hidden there, a piece of paper."

"Really? Hold on. I'll put you on speaker." I could hear her set the phone down and papers rustling. Following suit so that Sam could hear, I did the same and motioned to him to listen, as his ears had perked up when he heard me mention something hidden. "Hmm, I don't see anything. We've examined these pretty closely. The elk-skin cover appears intact. The only place anything could be hidden would be on the gathered edge, but it's so tightly bound I'd have to cut it open to check. I don't think we should do that, Kay. I'm sorry. I couldn't *possibly* cut into this."

I sighed, realizing that telling her I'd seen Tamahna in between worlds and she'd told me to look for Meriwether's letter in the binding would be a stretch for anyone. "I'm still the legal owner of the journals and letters," I reminded her. "I've only *loaned* them to the Smithsonian. I'm authorizing you to cut into that binding."

"Kay, you realize how irrational that sounds, right? These materials are a national treasure. It'd be criminal to deface one of them."

"Janet, if you don't do it, then I will. I can revoke the loan at any time—remember? I *know* that there's something there—something we missed. Trust me." Sam furrowed his brow, confused. As I waited for her to respond, I could imagine Janet deliberating. "OK, I'm typing up an e-mail right now, demanding to have the materials overnighted to me and the loan ending full stop," I told her.

"Wait!" Janet said. "OK, OK, OK! I'll do it, but I want it in writing. E-mail me the request, so when my boss asks, I can prove that you insisted that I cut into the binding."

"Deal." I typed out two sentences and sent it over. "Should be in your in-box now. I gave you full permission to deface a national treasure," I joked.

Janet was not amused. "OK, I see the e-mail," Janet replied, begrudgingly. "I still think this is reckless." She took a deep breath. "Here goes nothing," she said. "Something better be in here, Kay, because if you're wrong—"

"There will be. I just *know*." Sam and I waited anxiously.

"I'm cutting gently along the edge to be able to peel away the backing. I'm peeling some of the top section now," Janet said.

"It's like the golden days of radio," I joked to cut the tension. Sam laughed too.

"There's nothing—oh! Wait—there *is* something here, Kay. It's folded like an accordion. OK, I'm cutting all the way down the side now, and then I'll peel back the rest of this, so I can remove it in one piece safely, and we can repair the binding later. I can't believe this! It's like Christmas Day!" she exclaimed. "How did you know it was here?"

"I remembered something that Mom told me about the journals," I lied. "She mentioned a hidden document in the binding of the last one. I don't know what it is, but I believed her." Truth is stranger than fiction, and this story was plausible.

"OK…I'm unfolding it now, carefully, so it doesn't break into pieces. It might take me a few minutes. Want me to call you back, or do you want to stay on the line?"

"We'll stay," Sam quickly stated, and I smiled. We waited what seemed like hours until Janet spoke again.

"It's difficult to read, and it will take me a while to make sure I've gotten it right, but here's what it generally says at first glance. It's addressed to Jefferson from Meriwether." She scanned it quickly and relayed the main points. "Says Meriwether married an Indian woman named Anna, known locally as Tamahna, and he asks for special dispensation so that she is protected if anything should happen to him… that he wants to resign his service upon successful return to Missouri, when he will then leave to return to his wife in Cape Disappointment…asks to be released from duty…requests his ashes be returned to Cape Disappointment for ceremonial burial if he doesn't survive…Oh! And then I quote: 'Sir, I will most certainly disappoint you with my likewise refusal of undertaking a presidential election upon return as we discussed, your most loyal servant,' ending with his signature. Kay, do you realize what this means?"

I nodded and smiled. I knew it meant we had exactly what we needed to return him to Tamahna in the spirit world. "It means we can bring him home," I said. "I need your help to petition for his exhumation and the return of his ashes. With the DNA results and this letter, how could anyone refuse?"

"Kay…it's…this is," Janet sputtered. "I need to fully evaluate and authenticate this. When it comes back as authentic, then we'd have to engage with…someone about the exhumation. Although—prepare yourself—this will likely take years. I hate to ask you this, but would you approve a forensics examination of his remains? Results from forensics would help us to better understand how he died, whether it was a suicide or murder."

"Of course I'd support a forensics examination."

"What about the rest of the Lewis family?" Janet asked, clearly concerned about another family faction challenging my decision.

"Haven't you seen their web page? They'll support the examination."

"The web page?" Janet asked.

"And you call yourself an expert, professor. Believe me, the Lewis family wants to solve the mystery of Meriwether's death as much as we do."

"I'll check it out, and we'll order the forensics examination," she confirmed.

"OK, OK, do what you need to do, and call me when you have more information or need me to sign anything."

"I will, absolutely," Janet said.

"And Janet…"

"Yes?" she asked.

"Thanks for trusting me."

"Ditto," she said. "I'll be in touch soon."

Sam stared across the table. "You never mentioned any hidden document before, not to Lou or John. Kay, how did you know about that document?"

"I kind of learned about it more *recently*," I explained evasively.

"Like when you were…"

"In the veil…Tamahna told me about it."

"Oh," he said anxiously. "So straight from the source then."

"I don't want secrets between us. You and me—we're a team," I replied.

Sam leaned over to kiss me. "Yes, we are. And we'd be a *great* team sailing across the world."

"Ugh. Not that again," I scowled and threw my hands in the air. "What is it with you and this boat idea?"

"I want to be *alone* with you. No phones…No history mystery…No tsunamis."

I shook my head. "I'll see your yearlong tin-can-on-the-water seasick honeymoon and raise you a luxury resort in Hawaii."

"I fold. You win," he said.

"I think we *both* win."

I called Lou about the letter we'd discovered, and he was delighted, despite being distracted by baby Henry. He asked me to notify the Lewis family, whom we hadn't spoken with much since the DNA results had come back months earlier, although they had kindly invited us to their upcoming family reunion in September. We knew they'd be supportive of an exhumation, given the family's well-publicized efforts requesting one in order to use the latest scientific advances to determine whether or not Meriwether had been murdered. I agreed to speak with the Lewis side of the family and make sure they were included in the early findings that Janet promised to share with us. Before contacting them, though, I decided to take a break from the history mystery and spend the rest of the day with Sam at home.

"I'm sorry. I'm neglecting you with all this journal stuff," I said, curling up with him on the sofa.

"Yes, you are," he confirmed, removing his glasses. "Today is supposed to be *our* day. You've been gone a long time."

"I noticed that you painted Gran's room pink," I said.

"Yes, I did. So we're going to talk about that now...finally? I've been waiting a *month* for this conversation."

"I shouldn't have told you about our daughter," I said.

"I'm glad you did. It gave me hope that you would wake up and that we'd have a life together, despite your coma." He reached over for my hand.

"Still, I'm not going tell you anything more about it. It's not normal to know the future...or the hidden past, for that matter," I explained.

"Come on. It's *me*. You can tell me," he pestered, smoothing my hair. "And you did neglect me all morning."

I caved quickly. "I saw her playing with baby Henry, when he is about five years old, so it'll be a while yet. Besides, I still need to finish my internship and residency before we can even start to think about kids," I told him. He kissed me on the forehead.

"I'd like to name her Rosa, after my mom."

"I *might* have already promised to name her Saghalie," I countered guiltily. "I promised her, when we met in the veil—it just kind of came out. But, I think Saghalie Rosa Morandi is a lovely name."

Sam's eyes narrowed. He looked unhappy. "Kay, so you decided on the name of our daughter without consulting me? I don't want her stuck with a name no one can spell or pronounce. You can't make decisions like that without talking to me. We're supposed to be partners, making decisions *together*," he said angrily.

Now *I* was mad. "Partners? Like changing our wedding venue from the lighthouse to John's house? You made that decision completely without me."

"What? I *asked* you if you wanted to move it there."

"Oh, no, you didn't *ask*. You *told* me that he had offered it, and isn't that great...And Barry? I can't even make *coffee* in that starship of a kitchen!"

"Don't bring Barry into this! *You* chose *our* daughter's first name without consulting me," he argued.

"And *you* changed *our* wedding location to *Seaside*!" I replied. "Like I want to get married in Seaside! Generations of keelalles have married at the veil, and that's what we agreed."

Sam started to speak but stopped and then laughed. "Do you hear that?"

"What? What's so funny? Don't try and change the subject!"

"Listen...No thunder, lightning, hail, or trees falling down in the backyard."

"What?"

"We're fighting, and you're not taking it out on the town with the weather. Did you lose that...ability?"

"No, I learned how to control it. Holding back the tsunami was like learning to drive in a Ferrari at a hundred miles per hour on hairpin turns," I explained.

Sam laughed. "So we can be a normal couple who argues, and I don't have to worry about you destroying the town in a mad fury?"

I laughed too. "Yes, we can argue like normal couples now, only...right now, I don't want to...argue." I leaned in and kissed him.

"Me neither...I'm a lover, not a fighter," he whispered playfully, drawing me closer.

Alternatives ❧ *June*

*O*ur lives slowly returned to normal, with Sam working at the restaurant again, although he kept the other chef as well, which helped keep his hours flexible. I continued studying to cram med school back into my head before hitting the hospital while continuing to discuss the journals and discoveries with Janet whenever she called.

After my second cup of coffee and a mind full of flash cards, I took a break and walked up to the lighthouse. Breathing in the ocean breeze, I listened to the waves and recharged, watching the water roll across the beach below.

A bearded man sat down next to me, nodding in place of saying hello. "Lovely day out today, isn't it?" he stated.

"Yes," I responded, out of politeness.

"Excuse me, but are you Kay Baker? Sheila said I might be able to find you here. My name is Professor Amit Warner."

I sighed, annoyed to have my break time interrupted. "Yes, I'm Kay. And?" I prompted.

"I was hoping that I could talk to you about my research on the Cascadia earthquake. I'm a geophysics professor at Oregon State, and folks in town have suggested I meet you."

"I heard about you, asking questions around town," I confirmed.

"Then you have probably also heard that I don't agree with the other scientists who think Cascadia collapsed upon itself, which is why it didn't make landfall," he explained.

"Well then, what do you think happened? And why ask me?" I looked straight at him, seriously.

"There are Clatsop legends that say a medicine woman held back the Cascadia tsunami in 1700. Then there's the recent account of Jerry Reynolds who was out on his boat and witnessed the tsunami vanish into the ocean, noticing a woman on the cliff. Jerry thinks that was you, and, according to the Clatsop tribal council, *you* are their medicine woman."

"So you think I magically held the tsunami back? That sounds pretty difficult for most people to believe, don't you think? Besides, Jerry is hardly what anyone would call reliable."

"I'm more open minded than some of the other physicists in my department. The science they claim explains the collapse is bunk. A power resulting from a nine-point-three earthquake would require an equal opposing power for balance. So I'm open to alternative explanations. My grandmother grew up in Varanasi, India, and she taught me that there's always more than meets the eye," he said.

"Well, to believe that *one* person could stop a tsunami means you believe in *magic*, not science. I'm a physician and scientist myself," I replied.

"So you don't believe in magic like the rest of your tribe or the folks in town?" he asked.

"I believe in love," I replied simply.

"You didn't answer my question," he grumbled.

"Yes, I did. I'm sorry I can't be of more help, Professor. Enjoy the view," I said, standing up and walking away.

Wedding ❀ November

The whole wedding party arrived nearly a week ahead of the wedding, and most of them were staying at our house. As Sam had pointed out, that's exactly what big, old, drafty houses like ours were built for. Lou, Ashley, and baby Henry camped in Lou's old room, which we'd updated with a bigger bed and a crib; Sam's brothers Tony, Jack, and Mark stayed in Gran's old room because Sam thought it was funny for them to sleep in the pink room; Martina and Emma shared the pullout sofa in the office; and Sam's dad, Joe, slept in the converted attic room that had a winter view of the harbor and served as my painting studio.

John, Mary, James, and Betty from the tribe council commuted from their homes in nearby Seaside throughout the week, bringing up food dishes and anything we needed, like extra blankets, and general moral support. John took Sam's brothers and dad out ocean fishing in his boat for a day, and Mary stepped in as the mother figure, fussing about my dress and the flowers and taking pictures of everyone. Betty and Dorothy decorated the restaurant for the reception. Both Sam and I felt grateful to have them there as our extended family and knew we couldn't have managed the event and all the out-of-town guests without the tribe's help.

Kristin and Leon took Neb for the week because the house full of strangers was too much for Neb, and she was driving us up the wall. Sam closed the restaurant for a week to get the inventory done, change to a winter menu that focused on seasonal vegetables, and plan out the holiday events. It also gave Betty and Dorothy time to plan their decorations, and I couldn't have imagined a more dedicated pair of volunteer designers. However, I started to suspect they simply enjoyed being away from the boisterous house.

I worked early shifts in the hospital all week, minimizing time off from the program so we could take a week's honeymoon in Hawaii. To get all my hours in for the week and still be able to spend time with all the visitors, I started my day at four in the morning, arriving at the hospital by five. One morning, I shuffled quietly downstairs to get the coffee going, and I was startled to find Tony already downstairs, working on his laptop.

"You're up early," I observed. "Coffee?"

"Still some jet lag. Mark snores, so I figured I'd come down here for a while," he explained. "I'd love some coffee, thanks." I readied everything in my backpack and quickly pulled my hair back into a ponytail. "I noticed you're not using that big espresso machine," he said, acknowledging that instead of teaming up with Barry, I used the smaller, single-pot coffeemaker.

"Oh, yeah—Sam's the only one who knows how to get that to work. Barry is very fussy," I confirmed. "This little coffeemaker here is a compromise so I'm not left without coffee when he's not up yet. Although, honestly, this coffeemaker doesn't hold a candle to Barry." I laughed and Tony joined me.

"Barry is a little intimidating," he replied.

"I know, right? My theory is that Sam likes me relying upon him for coffee—a daily reminder that I'm hopeless without him. It's *true*, but don't tell him. Anyway, so you're already hard at work then, typing away?"

"Yes, well it's seven in New York, so prepping for when the markets open."

"Right, you're some sort of fund manager?"

"Yes, on Wall Street. And you're Morningside from Harlem? That painting you did of Sam is exceptional, the one in the restaurant. Are you still painting?"

"Gosh, I haven't been referred to as 'Morningside' in a year…Kind of took a break from painting. And right now with catching up on finishing my residency and, soon enough, the board exams, I haven't had much time for art," I explained, filling up his coffee mug. "I've been meaning to thank you all for coming over for the wedding. I know that your being here is very important to Sam."

"I wouldn't miss Sam's wedding. He's the best big brother a guy could have. Practically raised me and the others when Dad sort of checked out after Mom died. Sam even went to parent-teacher meetings for us at school, and he made sure we all went to college, although no one helped *him*. He worked full time when he was eighteen to help pay for us to go."

"I know. I'm so in love with that man." I looked at my watch, mindful of the time. "I'm sorry. I've got to run, so I can be back later this afternoon."

"Sure, I won't hold you up. I did want to tell you something, though. I know that Sam probably told you that I was worried about him marrying so quickly."

"Yeah, he did."

"I've never seen my brother so happy, not even with Rachel. Honestly, *now*, I don't know why he waited *so long* to marry you," Tony said, smiling.

I moved over to hug him gratefully. "Thank you for saying that," I said.

Martina, Emma, and I escaped to Kristin's the night before the wedding so we could hang out in Astoria together and have a girls' night out in the relatively "big city." Kristin was also adamant that the groom shouldn't see the bride before the wedding. Before we left the house, Sam pulled me aside in the driveway as everyone piled into Kristin's minivan.

As he swept me into his arms, I melted. "I'll see you tomorrow, missus," he whispered with a kiss.

"Yes, I'll be the one in white," I replied. He kissed me again, and his brothers hooted like rowdy frat boys from the doorway. Sam grinned.

"Have fun with the girls tonight," he said.

"I will—and try not to burn the house down," I said, glancing at his brothers while pushing his hair away from his face. Kristin honked the horn loudly, and I kissed Sam again quickly before getting into the car. This was our first night apart in several months, and it felt strange to know that I wouldn't see him until the following afternoon.

The girls and I went out for cocktails at the bistro under the bridge, the scene of my first date with Sam. Martina couldn't get over the *amazing* coincidence that she had hoped to hire Sam at her restaurant in New York, but then he had changed his mind at the last minute.

"He's the guy I wanted to set you up with, Kay. Remember? The guy I said was the spitting image of your painting? I just can't get over it. I keep staring at him, and he must think I'm nuts. He's an excellent chef too—exactly what you need, ramen girl. I'm dying to try that wine he recommended—the Yakima Valley Malbec he was raving about. Do they have it here?" she asked, seemingly possibly smitten with Sam herself. I smiled broadly, happy to finally have my friends approve of someone I was dating.

"Yes, they have it here. Shall we get a bottle, ladies?" I asked after our first round of gin and tonics. The vote was unanimous, in favor. "I've missed you all, and I do wish you lived closer, like Kristin here."

"I'd give anything to get out of Vermont," Emma complained.

"Not quite what you thought it would be?" Martina asked sympathetically.

"Not at all. Dr. Evans hired me because he wanted to diversify his practice by adding an osteopath, although he's such a total control freak and micromanager that I can't treat patients like an osteopath! It's so annoying, and I'm miserable all day and then a train wreck of bitter when I get home, making Ryan annoyed with me. All I want right now is to find a real osteo-pathic practice where I enjoy going to work each day. Sorry. This is Kay's big night, so let's drink to the bride, who has returned to medicine and met the perfect guy for her."

"Emma, you should think about moving here. Mom and Dad gave me the clinic in their will, but it's stood empty and will remain so until I finish my residency—unless you join the practice. You'd be on your own until I take the boards, but we could work together in our own osteopathic practice. Think about it," I suggested.

Emma smiled. "I will. Here's to Kay and Sam. Cheers!"

We clinked our glasses, and everyone raved about the wine. Martina pledged to extend her trip so she could drive to Yakima and arrange to add the wine to her restaurant's impec-cable wine list.

"I can't believe that only last year at this time you were with Adam, whom, it has to be said, *none* of us ever really liked. Am I right?" Emma's question was quickly met by nods of violent agreement from both Kristin and Martina. "But now, a year later you're living in a gorgeous, massive house in a beautiful fishing village, completing your residency, and getting married to Mr. Right. What a difference a year makes," said Emma.

If only they knew the half of it, I thought.

"And those brothers of his," Kristin commented. "I think they might be more in love with you than Sam, as if that were even possible."

"I wish I had the community of support you have around you, especially after your parents...have passed. I'm glad to see you are so well taken care of here," Martina said. "I didn't realize you were so involved with a tribe. You're suddenly this medicine woman related to Meriwether Lewis."

"Right—medicine woman, how apt!" Emma laughed, assuming it was a joke related to me being a doctor. I let it go, of course; even if they were my closest gal pals, I didn't feel the need to explain everything. Besides, I wouldn't even know where to start. After another bottle of wine, we took a taxi back to Kristin's house, where we soon ordered a pizza and continued gossiping well into the wee hours.

Our wedding day arrived, and there was enough love and joy in the air for me to influence a late-season heat wave that reached all the way to Idaho. Clear blue sky reflected the calm ocean waves, and the air was scented with roses, even though we decorated the chairs with irises. I knew Mom was there, by her signature scent. We wanted a small wedding, outside on the cliff beside the lighthouse. It was there that I'd first told Sam that I loved him, and it was also where we'd stood fast, holding back the Cascadia tsunami.

Two rows of ten chairs each and a simple platform to stand on at the front, near the cliff's edge, where the lowering sun reflected upon the water in shades of orange and pink—that was our perfect setting. Lou walked me down the aisle, and my attention focused entirely on Sam. We held hands, and Lou sat down.

John officiated, combining his role as chief and someone very close to both of us. Everything about the day felt natural and beautiful. John welcomed everyone and started with a few words.

"It is my privilege and honor to marry Sam and Kehlok today, on a beautiful day in this sacred place. Our people believe that the veil between worlds is thin here, and today I know that even the spirit world is celebrating this union. Anyone who has seen these two together knows that there is a powerful magic between Sam and Kehlok. When I first met them, Kehlok made it very clear that she wouldn't leave Sam out of anything—even our tribe." Everyone laughed. "And Sam included Kehlok in everything, even when she was in a coma, asking her which sandwich he should have for lunch or what she thought about a story he read in the newspaper." Everyone laughed again, although I could hear a few sniffles and tissues rustling. "They've prepared their own vows. Sam, do you have the ring?"

Sam smiled, placing a ring on my finger. "Kay, I've loved you since even *before* we met. I'll be your home, your safe harbor, your Americano maker, and I promise that I'll never let you go."

"Kay?" John prompted while I caught my breath, and Emma handed me Sam's ring to place on his finger.

"Sam, my heart is a river and you are the ocean. All my life has been a road to you. I give you my heart, and I promise to keep yours safe. I will love you forever." He leaned in to kiss me, without waiting for John to say the words *husband and wife*.

We spent a few hours at the reception party in the restaurant, leaving once the airport limo picked us up for our flight to a blissful week in Hawaii.

Big News ❈ *October*

$\mathcal{A}$lmost two years after our wedding, we piled onto the sofa to watch Janet discuss her book on the news. I leaned into Sam as he reached his arm across my shoulders, passing the bowl of popcorn.

"I wish we could have seen it live instead of the recording," I grumbled. "I feel like we never have enough time together, and I can't *wait* for my residency to be over next year. This schedule is brutal," I complained.

He smoothed my hair. "You're nearly done, Doc. Hang in there. Soon enough you can join Emma at the practice downtown and work normal hours."

"I know, but I miss you. We're both always working."

"Once I find someone to replace Mario, I'll be able to cut down on my hours again. It's only temporary. I miss you too." My heart swelled. "OK, I found it again. There she is." He pointed to the television, excitedly, as the segment began:

> *Host*: Tonight on the program, we welcome Professor Janet Cho of Georgetown University, who's been working with the Smithsonian on evaluating recently discovered

245

journals from the Lewis and Clark expedition. Her new book, entitled, *The Greatest Love Story Never Told*, is a best seller that sheds new light on Meriwether Lewis, a man we only *thought* we knew. Welcome, Professor Cho.

Cho: Thank you. I'm delighted to be here.

Host: Can you summarize the revelations about Meriwether Lewis that your research has uncovered from these new materials?

Cho: Most importantly, the new information indicates that hundreds of his journal entries were removed before the original publication of the journals. We've also learned that Meriwether married a Clatsop medicine woman and planned to return to her after the completion of the discovery mission. In many ways, their relationship is the greatest love story never told, and it threw new light on his death and provided enough evidence to sponsor his exhumation for a formal forensics evaluation.

Host: That's something the Lewis family has lobbied for, isn't that right?

Cho: Yes, for many years they've wanted to solve the mystery, and these missing entries helped further their legal case as well as the identification of his direct descendants. And the forensics evaluation was compelling,

proving without a doubt that he was murdered and didn't commit suicide as previously
thought.

Host: Professor Cho, who do you think murdered Meriwether Lewis?

Cho: That's a two-hundred-year-old question
that we might never learn the answer, however, at least people are asking the question now.

I exhaled deeply and beamed. "We did it," I said.

"*You* did it, coyote girl. He's vindicated after two hundred
years—amazing! And Janet's changed history, literally rewritten it," Sam said.

"*We've* rewritten it. I wouldn't have found those journals
without the snowdrops you kept bringing me," I reminded him.

"I *am* your hero, aren't I?" he stated proudly.

"Always," I replied with a kiss. "Do you really want to
watch this whole program now or...later?" I asked.

"*Definitely* later," he quickly replied, turning off the TV and
pulling me close.

Homecoming ❦ *January*

eturning home late after another long day at the hospital, I fell into bed, exhausted. Sam had waited up for me.

"Is the morning sickness at least going away?" he asked, concerned. "You shouldn't be working this hard right now."

"I desperately miss sleep, and these last few months of any residency are tough. I'm almost done, though, and this baby's mom will be an official doctor," I replied.

"Olivia? Or what about Anne?" he asked. We had agreed that Saghalie Rose would be the baby's middle names, allowing us to meet family obligations while still giving our daughter a name of her own.

I sighed heavily and yawned. "Anne? Are we starting over on the "A" names again? I thought we both liked Olivia?"

"No, my first girlfriend was Olivia, remember?"

I groaned. It seemed as if we'd never agree on a name. "We have until August to decide. I'm too tired to have this conversation."

"Oh, I almost forgot. Janet's package arrived today, sent express mail. Must be a box of books. I had to sign for it."

I knew it wasn't books. "It's...Meriwether! They finished all the forensic tests—remember? Oh, come on. We have to go to the veil."

"What? Can't it wait until tomorrow? You're beat, and I'm already in bed," he argued.

Yawning again, I sat up and pulled his arm. "No, it can't wait. They've been separated for two hundred years, and I won't make them wait another minute. Come on. Get dressed. What if it was us? Would you want someone to wait *another* day before reuniting *us?*"

He kissed me on the cheek. "Well, when you put it that way...Let me get dressed."

I went downstairs to open the box. Pulling out the urn carefully encased in a plastic box and sealed with tape, I set it on the kitchen counter. "Hello, Meriwether. We're taking you home," I said.

Sam's footsteps trudged steadily toward me. "Hmm...I thought he'd be...*taller*," Sam joked. I laughed so hard I coughed. I couldn't remember feeling more tired, and I knew Sam was too; yet there we were on a frozen winter night, driving to the lighthouse.

Only the stars and the lighthouse lit up the dark sky. The bitter wind slapped our faces when we stepped outside the car. Sam grimaced at the cold, looked into my eyes knowingly, and held my hand and kissed me. I closed my eyes and took a deep breath, focusing my energy on calming the wind. Instantly, the wind paused, slowed, and shifted toward the sea.

"Now, *that's* what I'm talking about," Sam said, moving both of his hands to warm my face. "Without the wind, it's not too bad out here tonight."

"Come on. We won't be out here long." I took his hand as we walked with Meriwether's urn to the cliff's edge. I shifted the winds again to move the ashes through the veil as I had done for Mom, Dad, and Gran several years earlier.

"Do we say something? Maybe play *taps* from my phone?" Sam asked.

"We say good-bye and send him to the spirit world." I opened the top of the urn as the ashes started floating up along the wind. "Go find Tamahna, Meriwether. She's waiting for you," I whispered.

"Just follow the ocean," Sam whispered. "Find your girl." Sam put his hand on my back as we watched the ashes disappear into the darkness. Before turning away, we saw two shooting stars stream brightly across the sky toward each other. I could feel joy and love emanate from the veil.

"Look! They found each other," I said, watching the stars merge together.

Sam shouted into the wind, "Way to go, Meriwether!" He turned to me, his face next to mine, making my heart skip a beat. "What about 'Meredith'?" he asked suddenly. "It's her *own* name but still a form of Meriwether."

"Yes, that's perfect—Meredith Saghalie Rose Morandi," I agreed. "Baby finally has a name," I said with relief.

He kissed me. "Let's go home, amore mio."

About the Author

Julie Manthey started writing stories for her family and friends as soon as she could hold on to a crayon. She is a proud Hoya alumna of Georgetown University.

Julie is an independent author and has self-published this book. If you enjoyed reading it, please, tell *all* your friends and consider writing a review on Amazon or Goodreads. Thanks for your support!

HeyJoule.WordPress.com

Made in the USA
Charleston, SC
08 January 2016